How I Found Myself Naked in the Footlights

by
Jamie Alexandre Hall

Auctoritas

JAMIE ALEXANDRE HALL

Cover art by Justin Evangelista ©2012

ISBN-10: 0985801751
ISBN-13: 978-0-9858017-5-5

AUCTORITAS PUBLISHING LLC
848 S. Kimbrough
Springfield, MO 65806

DEDICATION

TO MOM

Table of Contents

CHAPTER ONE

How I Got To Where I Was Going

"Matthew, I never told you anything about your father, did I?"

The rain had been pouring down for an hour or two before I got off the bus, and the temperature outdoors was nearly freezing. But, as they say, desperate men do desperate things – even braving a cold, rainy day without a proper jacket.

I stepped from the comparative warmth of the bus, dragging two unwieldy suitcases, and surveyed my surroundings as the bus roared away down the road. There wasn't much to it, really. Just a sign post and a bench which were both so rickety and old that I doubted either one of them would hold my weight if I tried to rest against one of them. And it was then, looking at the result of my poorly-planned excursion, that the thing that had set off all of this was slammed fully into my mind: "Matthew, I never told you anything about your father, did I?"

The rural surroundings dropped away from me – and I was back at my desk in Chicago. In that moment, it was as if all the random chatter of city life had ceased; all the car horns blaring, all the people yelling. Even my office seemed to fall silent, and I found I was gripping the sheet of yellow legal pad paper so hard that my fingers were turning white.

"I don't seem to remember doing so, but goodness knows I always meant to do it someday. And since the doctors say this thing is inoperable now, I decided that I'd finally just gather up my nerve and tell you all, but... well, you know! I tried to bring it up, but it seemed like it was such a big embarrassing fuss, and you know I hate fusses. I know you'll be going through my papers after I go, so..."

I remember pausing, wondering if maybe I ought to put away this letter until some other time -- some other time when I could have a chance to prepare myself. But I'd had it in the drawer of my desk at work for two weeks now, waiting for the right moment, trying to prepare myself for whatever the nondescript envelope might hold. But the longer I waited, the larger the envelope had seemed to grow in my mind until I was just sitting at my computer and staring at the desk drawer, my fingers beating a staccato on the desktop.

I *had* to read it. I *had* to finish it at that moment if I ever wanted to put some closure on Mom's passing. But this... this wasn't what I had bargained for. Swallowing dryly, I held it in shaking hands in the blue light of my computer monitor.

"Matthew, honey, I guess I'll just say it. Henry Dale Kitteridge, Mosstone, Devonshire, England. That's your father. This is all I wanted to say -- I just wanted to you know his name, and where he was living when I last heard from him. Well, toodle-oo and see you much, much, much later..."

She had signed the letter her full name, then added in parentheses, in case I didn't get it, "*Your Mother*".

Ah yes. That was very Mom.

I had never asked Mom about my father. Asking about it seemed to be asking for some big, dramatic scene with crying and beating on chests – and if there was one thing I inherited from Mom, it was a dislike of *scenes*. Mom and I didn't like upsetting people or being upset. We were a pair of quiet, circumspect people who always hated drama and the limelight. But I did wonder.

Perhaps it was the constant question, "What *are* you?" that seemed to plague my childhood. My skin was too dark for me to be a Caucasian – too light to be an African American. I have thick, unwieldy, inconsistently curling black hair, so you could probably call me Hispanic or Indian – except for the fact that I have an incredibly square, Anglo face, and my eyes are an unnatural-looking green. Oh, and I have freckles. In short, I look like nothing on earth. So when the kids asked me, "What are you?" I generally responded with, "Eskimo". Nobody knows anything about Eskimos, so that usually ended the conversation.

But that didn't answer *my* questions. Who was I, really? The repeated question of my peers was simply an external echo of the internal voice that reverberated around my mind. Even during the brief times in my life that the question was muted, it didn't stop the inevitable questions. I was still what-are-you'd by people, still teased, still tormented.

The harshest of my childhood tormentors was a skinny, redheaded girl named Patty Lloyd. Acting out on some latent masochistic tendencies, and because I like women who know what they're about, I wound up dating Patty for a long while. After college Patty wanted to get married, but I didn't feel it was the right time, so she ditched me and married a surgeon named Frank. I don't blame her, and Frank's a wonderful guy, so Patty and I remained friends. She and Frank are probably my closest friends now, so when this yellow, unsettling, last letter from my mother came to my hands, it was Patty that I went to for advice.

"Henry Dale Kitteridge?" Patty said, blinking her big round eyes as if the name had struck a familiar chord.

"Don't tell me you recognize it."

"Not in the slightest. So who is he?"

I shrugged. "No idea."

"You mean the letter didn't give any other information about him? Just his name and a town he used to live in?"

I shrugged. "Yup."

"Well, what are you going to do about it?"

I put down a glass of milk that I'd been draining and wiped my mouth on the back of my hand. "That's what I was going to ask you. I don't know what to do about it."

"Did you look for him on the internet?"

I rolled my eyes. What a question to ask an IT guy.

"Okay, well, what did you find then, genius?"

"I found a couple Henry Dale Kitteridges in the world - but not one in Mosstone England. Then I just tried to find out some information on Mosstone, and came up short there too; it doesn't even have its own website. The closest thing I could find was a blurb on the British Tourism site: 'Quaint, rustic town, notable for having been the home of…'"

Patty waited. "The home of what?"

"It didn't say. Apparently the person writing the blurb lost interest."

She grunted. "That's encouraging."

Frank, who was sitting in the center of the kitchen floor putting together a large puzzle, looked up at me with drooping eyes. "Matt, I hope you realize that this might be a dead end. The seventies were a long time ago; he could have moved. He could have changed his name. Or…"

"Or he could have given her a fake name," Patty added, with a raised eyebrow.

"Patty!"

"Well, it *has* been known to happen," Patty said, frowning at me seriously, "especially in situations like this."

"Give her a little credit," I grabbed a chocolate chip cookie off a plate on the table and jammed it in my mouth, chewing with difficulty. "Mom was a smart woman. I don't see her getting taken in by a con man – and I don't see her getting involved in the first place with the kind of… of *scoundrel* who would give her a false name and then ditch her. I just don't see it."

"Scoundrel," Frank repeated, holding up a puzzle piece to the light and closing one eye as he examined it. "That's a good word. People don't use it enough."

Patty lowered her eyes for a moment, then reached across the table and took my hand with an expression usually reserved for retarded puppies.

"Matt," she said gently, "I'm going to say this because you're like the ethnically diverse half-brother I never had, okay?"

I hesitated. "Okay?"

"There is *some* reason why your parents didn't stay together. And *some* reason why your father was never involved in your life. I'm going to say that it's a safe bet that there was something seriously wrong with the situation if thirty something years have passed and this is the first you've heard about him!"

I lowered my eyes and swallowed hard jagged chunks of the cookie. Then I took a deep breath and said, "I think I have to go to England and find him."

"Matt," Patty said with a warning note in her voice.

"Look," I said plaintively, "I might at least find somebody who knew him. Or I might find his family. I might have grandparents, aunts, uncles, brothers and sisters that I never knew about! It boggles the mind!"

"Then again," Frank said, pressing the puzzle piece into place, "you might spend a lot of money, waste a lot of time, and come home with absolutely nothing to show for it."

"Well, yes, that's an option too." I picked up another cookie and almost cracked a tooth trying to bite it in half. "Jeez, how old are these things?"

"Not *that* old," Patty remarked, picking one up and sniffing it.

I took a deep breath. "I think I have to do this."

Patty always has to take the pessimistic view of things. She picked up her sandwich and picked at it for a moment, then put it down and wiped her hands on the tablecloth. She and Frank exchanged a look, and then she folded her arms and sat back, shaking her head.

"Well, Matthew Henry Evans," she said, "I certainly hope you know what you're doing."

I felt myself grinning. I had Pat's permission. "Of course I do. I've left you in charge of sorting through her stuff, haven't I?"

"You know what I mean. This might seem like a good idea now, in a nice, comfortable kitchen with milk and cookies in front of you, but when you get there," she paused and raised an eyebrow at me significantly, "you're going to lose your nerve."

I shut my eyes. "Patricia --"

"You know what I'm talking about. I *know* you. If you had any gumption in the first place, you'd have asked me to marry you before Frank did! No offense, Frank."

"None taken, dearest."

"When you find him – *if* you find him – I cannot see you marching up to a total stranger and announcing that you're his long-lost son. As I recall, you're the guy who would rather give a taxi-driver a twenty dollar tip than ask for change." She paused. "Tell me I'm wrong. Go ahead. Tell me. Even *Frank* has more balls than that. No offense, Frank."

"I took that one as a compliment, actually."

This was getting far too personal and far too much like a *scene*. I looked up at the ceiling and thrummed my fingers on the tabletop.

"Look, Pat, I'm not going to argue with you --"

"You just proved my point, bucko."

I took a deep breath and fished for my keys in my pocket. "-- I'm going to England to find my Dad, and nothing is going to stop me. Not even *me!*"

"I'm from Missouri," Patty said firmly, then tossed a cookie to Frank.

* * *

The doubts Patty and Frank had voiced were issues that had already occurred to me. What if this was just a waste of time? Or what if I did find him – and I couldn't bring myself to talk to him? I let these worries dog at me, stew in my stomach and gnaw at my brain until a week later when I was sitting alone in my apartment, watching Chaplin's *The Kid* with the lights out. I chewed my nails and tugged my hair until it reached that moment when the child is crying and reaching out his little arms and crying out *"Daddy! Daddy!"* - and I leapt up off the couch, ran to my computer and booked a plane ticket for the next day.

On November third -- a foggy, rainy, uninviting morning -- I arrived in the town of Mosstone, Devonshire, England.

CHAPTER TWO

An Extremely Brief Search

Mosstone, Devonshire. A small, rustic town with a tiny, cobbled town square – surrounded by miles and miles of farmland. I wish I could say that, as I marched down that narrow, winding, muddy road, I enjoyed the sight of the rolling farmland, the cows, the sparse patches of trees – the strangely alien, manicured feeling of a countryside that has been densely inhabited for thousands of years – the majestic clouds rolling across the sky like the ghosts of giants.

But all I could think about was how cold I was, and what a fool I had been to fly to England in November without an umbrella.

I tried to ignore the ice-cold raindrops going down my neck and trickling down my back; I tried to ignore the fact that thousands of sharp little icicles were forming on the kinks in my hair; I even tried to ignore the fact that I was sinking in the icy mud up to the top of my sneakers. But I couldn't ignore the fact that my hands – my bare, cold, wet hands – were going numb and releasing the handles of my suitcases every few moments. I'd take a couple steps and then – plop! – I'd hear the suitcases drop into the mud beside me. Then I would turn around, rub my hands together until some slight sense of feeling had returned to them, clamp them around the suitcase handles again and take another couple steps before repeating the process.

When I finally arrived at the town square, it was with an intense wave of relief. Civilization at last! I washed the caked mud off my shoes in an icy puddle of water, then ran to the nearest awning for some relief from the rain and tried to figure out where I ought to start.

I must admit that, standing under the blue awning, was where I began to feel my first moment of anxiety. A little grocery store called McIntyre and Sons; a pub called "The White Stag", a post office and a library. Where should I start? *And what should I say?* I couldn't very well just walk in and say, "I'm looking for my long-lost illegitimate father – have you seen him?"

At the mere thought of that I shut my eyes, experiencing a moment of profound dread. Finally, I swallowed dryly. I *had* to do this – I had to. If I gave up now, Patty would never let me live it down. That alone forced me to pry my eyes open.

Okay, I reasoned. I didn't have to ask for my father. I could just ask if anybody had ever heard of Henry Dale Kitteridge. If they wanted to know *why* I was asking about him… I'd say I was doing genealogical research. It was kind of true. I squared my shoulders and marched out from under my protection to the building on the corner – McIntyre and Sons.

Mr. McIntyre was a tall, athletic looking old man with a long white mustache and very slick white hair. He held up his glasses in front of his face while I talked, and then said absently, "Henry Kitteridge? Yes, of course I know Henry. Say, would you be wanting some milk?"

I went weak at the knees. I really had not expected the first person I saw to say yes. I had expected hemming and hawing, or maybe – at best – a, *Henry Kitteridge? Oh, he died ten years ago.*

"He *is* alive, then?" I said, my voice quavering.

"Unless he's thrown himself under a car since he danced in here this morning, I'd say it's more than likely. Say, would you like some bacon? I got some lovely bacon."

I couldn't believe it. Had Henry Dale Kitteridge really in this village for the past thirty one years? Maybe he was just waiting for me to come and find him! I looked around the little dark room with a bubbling new respect. My *father* had actually been inside this room, perhaps just a couple of hours before. I wanted to sing – or throw up – or maybe a combination of the two. While I stood there considering the issue, Mr. McIntyre grew impatient.

"Look here, young feller – I'm a busy man, and I ain't got time to waste. Do you want me bacon or not?"

"Yes, yes," I said, dreamily, "I'll take some."

"'Ow much?"

"A pound?"

"A pound's worth or a pound of bacon?"

"Oh, uh – a pound of bacon."

As he wrapped my pound of bacon in white wax paper, I gradually came to my senses. I needed more details.

"Say, do you know where Mr. Kitteridge is now? I... I need to talk to him about something."

Mr. McIntyre stared at the ceiling for the longest time, as if he'd only just noticed it was there and it rather startled him. I was driven out of my mind before he finally replied, "No, I'm not quite sure where old Henry would be. It seems to me that he told me where he would be later this afternoon, and it seems to me that it was important at the time, but I can't seem to think of it. You might try the Post Office – they'd know."

Thanking him profusely as I paid for my pound of fatty white bacon, I turned and bolted from the store, awkwardly tucking the package under my arm. Between chafing wet feet, two un-wieldy bags and the bacon under my arm, it was a difficult waddle down the street to the Post Office, but I made it.

There was a short line. I dropped my bags by the door and waited impatiently. When I finally made it up to the stout, red-headed woman at the counter, I was keenly aware of the other parts of me that had warmed and begun to chafe inside my wet clothes; it was with an unhappy expression that I dropped my bacon on the lady's counter and gently asked if she could tell me where Henry lived. When I finished my question she looked at me as if there was a squirrel crawling out of my eye.

"Give you private information about the household of a postal customer?!" she snapped, standing up sharply and waving me away from her. "I don't think so. Move along, please."

"But, please," I said, surrendering my spot to an elderly woman who appeared to be mailing a bowling ball to France, "I really do need to find him…"

"I don't give out private information about postal customers," she snapped, weighing the bowling ball. "And especially not Henry Kitteridge!"

She gave me such a fierce look at that point that I grabbed my bacon and shot out of the building.

I skidded to a stop under the next awning and stood there, intimidated, trying to figure out what that experience meant. Was she just mad at me because I was a foreigner who seemed to be prying for information about the locals?

My two bags suddenly landed on the pavement beside me. The fierce woman was leaning out the door of the post office, almost shaking her fist at me.

"And if you find him, you tell Mr. Henry Dale Kitteridge to pick up his mail! This is a post office – not a place for him to store his bills!"

She ducked back inside and slammed the door behind her.

I think I shuddered slightly at this point… and it wasn't merely that I was back in the cold. The words, *This does not bode well* appeared in my mind, but I immediately tried to suppress them. I mustn't become discouraged. I mustn't let myself… think… because if I thought about the implications of what had just happened, I would see Henry Dale Kitteridge in my mind as a horrible, non-bill-paying, post-office-irritating slob of a man – not the sort of person I would want to call family. If I thought about this too much I would wind up turning around and going home, and I couldn't do that.

I picked up my bags and marched back down the street to the pub, the White Stag. If they didn't know where Henry was, at least they might be able to tell me where I could get a room for the night. It was beginning to get dark out, and I had a feeling that this might take a while.

I was wrong on that point.

The barkeep, an older man with a large, red nose and wispy hair, snapped his fingers after I asked my question.

"Wait – I know." He snapped his fingers again. "The church. Go down the highway a ways and you'll see it. St. Stephen's. That's where you'll find your man."

The church? The implications gave me a startling new image of my father: a gentle, pious white-haired man kneeling at the pew in a sunlit country chapel. He'd been a bit wild in his youth, but now he was sorry for it and spent his days in quiet contemplation. I could deal with a father like that.

"You did hear what I said?" I gulped, afraid he'd mis-heard, afraid I would be disappointed. "Henry Dale Kitteridge."

"Aye, I heard ye, young man. And I said you'd find him at St. Stephen's. We're great fans of Henry's round here, and we should know where he is. But when you see him – you tell him I'd appreciate it if he'd come by and settle up his bill. Just remind him friendly-like."

I turned around and ran out of there like a shot, splattering down the side of the highway. It was awkward going with the bacon tucked under my arm, my hands exhausted from switching my suitcases back and forth – but I was so intent on my goal I hardly noticed.

Finally, I spotted the church – a quaint little stone building with ornate wooden doors. I ran up to it, water splashing around my feet, and irreverently threw a door open, heaving myself inside and dropping my wet bags on the floor.

I found myself in a snug little entryway. It had dark brown walls and an extremely thick red carpet that completely muffled the sound of my footfalls. There was a yellow, ill-looking potted palm in one corner, and curtains over two arched doorways. There was a soft sound of several people speaking coming from behind the curtain, so I immediately took a step toward them --

"Hey!" a girlish voice behind me shouted. "Do you have a ticket?"

I whirled around and found a card table with a gum-smacking teenage girl sitting at it. She pouted at me, most displeased.

"Oh, uh," I said, walking back slowly and feeling embarrassed, wondering why I had to buy a ticket to go to church. "Um, I'll have one, please." As she made my change, I finally asked, "What is it for?"

"Don't you know? You seemed pretty eager to get in for a fellow who doesn't know what play is on..."

Oh! They were putting on a church play! How nice and quaint and... well, quaint. I shook myself.

"Well, actually I'm looking for someone. Do you know where a Mr. Henry Dale Kitteridge is?"

She smirked at me and pointed at the poster again. The ink-jet printed poster read, "The Princess and the Pea" and under that there was a list of names -- at the end of which, standing out in big bold red writing:

Written, Directed and Produced
by Henry Kitteridge.

A poster has never given me chills before.

I nervously chewed my thumbnail, suddenly wondering what on earth I was going to say to him. I steeled myself and gathered what shreds of courage I still had.

"Listen," the girl suddenly said, shrugging at me, "I changed my mind. Don't bother paying -- the panto's almost over, anyway. No charge."

"Thanks!" I cried, then pushed aside the curtain and stepped through the doorway. The show was going on up in the back of the church. It was ending. A girl with a small crown (apparently the Prince) and a girl with a pointy hat on her head (apparently the Princess) were standing together next to a pile of mattresses, while a fellow with a large crown (apparently a King) was pulling what appeared to be a squashed green pea out from under the bottom mattress and looking amazed, while a pantomime horse danced across the stage...

My eyes swept over the faces of the actors. Was Henry one of the motley crew on stage, or was he one of the six or seven people sitting unenthusiastically in the pews? The King was a tall man with a gray beard -- he looked like he might be old enough to be the parent in question – but he... Well, he didn't look like me.

The other man on stage was a girl, which only left the horse – and there was no way of knowing about the contents of that animal. I put my thumbnail to my teeth again, giving it an anxious chew. Where was Henry Kitteridge? My momentary burst of elation was being rapidly swapped for anxiety. What if he wasn't here? What if the barkeep had been wrong? What if everybody was wrong and this Henry Kitteridge wasn't even the *right* Henry Kitteridge? How could I possibly know?

All I can say about the next few minutes is *thank goodness* I didn't have long to wait before the pantomime ended – or I would have entirely lost my nerve. A couple moments later the cast was taking its bows. They got a patter of unenthusiastic applause from the pews, then the audience began to leave and the cast filtered off the stage.

I watched the people who left the theatre… A man in a battered cap, an old woman with a cane. Men who looked nothing like me – men who I couldn't see my mother falling in love with. Finally, they were all gone except for one man, a small, white-haired man, kneeling in the pew – his head down in prayer.

My heart was threatening to cram itself into my throat and choke me to death.

I took a step towards him – then another, and then finally I stood at his side. Before I quite realized what I was doing my voice quavered out – "Father?"

He looked up. "Yes, my son?"

The next thing I knew I was lying flat on the floor between the pews, and the old man was fanning my face with a handkerchief while the teenage girl snapped her gum at me.

"Oh, he's coming to," the old gentleman said, a relieved look on his face. "Young man – young man. Can you hear me, my son?"

My mind was blurry. The back of my head hurt; I must have hit a pew on the way down. I looked up at the man. There he was – my Dad. He didn't look *much* like me, but I supposed I could see a resemblance around the mouth… "Father…"

"I'm Father Douglas Ainsley," he said, loudly, as if he was talking to someone who was deaf. "Are you ill? Can I get you a glass of water?"

My eyes slipped down his face to the white collar at his throat.

Oh… he was *that* kind of father…

"Father Douglas," I repeated, and then reached for the edge of the pew to pull myself up.

"Stay down, my son – you've had a nasty fall."

"I'm fine, really," I said, pulling myself shakily to my feet. "I'm sorry… It's been a long day. I just got off a plane from America two

22

hours ago… I guess I haven't slept in like twenty four hours…"

"Oh, an American!" Father Douglas said, clapping his hands together. "How nice. I went to America once when I was a young man."

I choked slightly. "You *did?*"

"Yes, my parents took me to New York to visit an aunt when I was about five. I always wanted to go back again… Are you sure you don't want to sit down for a bit? Gladys, get this young man a glass of water."

"No, really, I'm fine," I said, feeling my cheeks flush with embarrassment as the girl padded off to the back of the church.

"Please, please, humor an old man – have a seat for a minute and wait for that glass of water. There, that's a good fellow. Now, tell me where in America you're from, and what on earth you're doing in Mosstone?"

"I'm from Chicago, and…" I swallowed and gave my half-truthful answer. "…And I'm doing some family research."

"Really! Genealogy is a fascinating subject. You know, you've come to the right place – I have records here dating back hundreds of years. If you'd like to come to my office, I can show you records of christenings and funerals that date back to—"

I couldn't get sidetracked: not now, not so close to my goal. I rudely interrupted him and said, "I'm sorry, Father, I actually came here to meet somebody."

He raised his eyebrows. "Well, perhaps I can direct you to the individual. What is the name?"

"Henry Dale Kitteridge."

The smile faded from his face.

"Oh. I see." He sniffed, turning away slightly. "You know, I don't approve of these silly shows being put on inside the church: I only let them move it in here on account of the rain." He sniffed again. "Well, you'll find him back there – in the vestibule."

I thanked him and heaved myself, running towards the vestibule shakily.

"Wait, my son!   You dropped your bacon!"

I pretended I hadn't heard. The doorway was covered by another one of those thick curtains, which I threw aside – running full into the chest of the gray-bearded man who had played King. He had been peeling off his costume, and seemed rather irked at me for knocking him off his feet.

"Excuse me," I said, my voice high-pitched and shaky as I helped him back up, "are you... Henry Dale Kitteridge?" (I almost said, "...my father?")

"No!" he said sharply, answering both versions of my question, and shoved past me muttering, "Damn Yanks think they can go barging in anywhere they please..."

I continued into the dark, crowded room, and looked around. The cast was standing about, changing out of their costumes into street clothes. I was embarrassed – I wanted to run away, back to the bus and straight back to the airport. But instead I summoned all that was left of my strength and marched right up to the first person I saw (a tall, gawky, pimple-faced teenage boy), and spoke. "Would you point me at Henry Dale Kitteridge?"

 He was another one of these droopy-jawed, slow-thinking types, but mercifully it wasn't too terribly long before he lifted a bony finger and pointed over toward a group of people undressing on the other side of the room. I thanked him, then swallowed very hard and shakily marched over.

As I got closer I examined the group and noticed that none of the men was old enough to be my father. The kid must have misunderstood. Fate seemed to have quit working for me and begun conspiring against me.

I walked up to the old lady -- a short, ugly old thing with ridiculously painted cheeks and a frizzy bright red wig on her head.

She was in the process of undoing the front of her dress, so I decided to ask here where Dad was before she got any further.

"Excuse me, ma'am," I said, "can you tell me where Henry Kitteridge is?"

She lifted up her painted face and took a look at me. I got a strong sour whiff of smoker's breath.

"Who did you say you were looking for?" she cackled.

"Henry Dale Kitteridge. He's supposed to be involved in this play, and I rather need to speak to him about, uh, something..."

"I'm Henry Kitteridge," she said, pulling off her wig and revealing the short silver hair underneath. She unzipped the dress and dropped it to her ankles; underneath she was dressed in a white shirt, brown trousers and black socks.

She was a man.

He stepped out of the dress and hung it on a nail on the wall, then picked up a damp rag from the table and began scrubbing the stage-paint off his white little face. "What did you want? Come on, speak up – I haven't got all day."

I attempted to speak, but I just choked on the words. He was dressed like a *woman*! There had to be some kind of mistake here... This couldn't possibly be him...

"Oh, I know who you are!" he suddenly said, smiling and shaking his finger at me.

"You *do?*" I choked.

"You're that young man from the village who was supposed to come around and clean up after the show! Well, you're a day late, young man, and you're not getting paid for yesterday – that's certain. Go out and sweep up between the pews so the vicar doesn't get his knickers in a twist – then come back in here and pack up these costumes."

"But – but..."

"Hurry up, then!" He jammed an old broom into my hands. "Get a move on, or I shan't be paying you for today either." He clapped his hands. "Spit spot."

I turned and walked out of the vestibule in a daze with the broom in my hand. I looked around the church vaguely, looked down at the broom – and started sweeping.

What can I say? I didn't quite have the presence of mind to explain that I wasn't the cleaning boy. I couldn't believe that I had actually just met my real father, and that he had been in drag... It just made my brain break down.

As I scooped dust into an ashcan in the front of the church, I comforted myself that he looked much less like a woman without the makeup on. After all, men dressing up as women are a tradition in British Pantomime plays, aren't they?

But that wasn't what really bothered me. The question *'Why on earth didn't he recognize me?'* kept running through my mind. Maybe it was irrational. But on some level I had expected him to look at me and know. I expected him to throw his arms out and cry, "My son! At last!" and embrace me.

Instead, there I stood, an old battered broom in my hands – and probably a pretty stupid look on my face. Was it really him? Maybe I'd made a mistake.

I had to talk to him. By the time I finally regained enough clarity of thought to attempt such a thing, the church was empty. Henry Dale Kitteridge had gone. I rushed out of the church into the muddy road, but he was nowhere to be seen.

* * *

I found out where Henry lived from Father Douglas, and set off. The sun was going down by this time, and I was worried about finding the place – but it wasn't difficult.

The Kitteridge residence was a decrepit little stone house surrounded by cattle pastures. The fence hadn't been painted extremely recently; there was a rusting bicycle against the gate, and there were flower gardens overgrown with dead brown weeds. If I hadn't known better, I would have said that the place was abandoned.

What was I going to say to him? Perhaps I should just come right out – *Mr. Kitteridge, I'm your son. My name is Matthew Henry Evans.*

Feeling a bit queasy, I walked slowly up the little stone walkway, dragging my suitcases with blistered hands.

I stood on that step for a good five minutes before I finally got the nerve up to ring the bell; after which I immediately turned, ran, and hid in the bushes.

After a few minutes I went back and rang it again, this time staying until he answered it.

The door swung opened a few inches inward and Henry Dale Kitteridge peered out at me suspiciously. I could hear the Bee Gees *Stayin' Alive* playing loudly inside his house.

"Yes?" he snapped.

"I – uh…" My voice caught in my throat. I just stared at him.

Silver gray hair. Square, very British face. Small mouth, Roman nose. *My nose.*

"Oh, it's you," Henry said, a look of displeasure on his face. He opened the door and reached for his wallet. "I must have forgotten. How much was it we agreed upon?"

Every word that I might have said instantly vanished from my head.

He was standing there, wallet in hand, staring at me with arched eyebrows. "Well? How much?"

"I'm…" My palms went damp. "I'm not here about that."

"Oh?" He put his wallet away hastily, and then a look of suspicion crawled across his face. "Then who are you? If this is about that fire –"

"No," I said, hastily.

"Then it must be that tab? You can just tell old Jenks that Henry Dale Kitteridge keeps his word – he'll be paid first of the month."

"It's not about that," I said, struggling.

"Are you from the gas company?"

"No."

"Are you from the Police?"

"No," I said, desperately.

He looked me up and down. "You're not here to break my legs, are you?"

"No!" I cried, desperately.

"Then who are you, man? Speak up, speak up."

"Mr. Kitteridge – I'm… your…" The word *son* would not come out of my mouth. "I'm… a relative... of sorts."

He turned his face away and waved a wrist at me airily. "Pshaw. I have no relatives, and certainly no American relatives. Look, if you're selling something, you can keep it. And now, sir, I must inform you that I am far too busy for idle chit-chat, so I bid you good day."

He slammed the door in my face.

My hope died. I had come all this way, beaten incredible odds to find my father, and been rejected by him all in the course of about two hours. All that was left was for me to go home in disgrace and spend the rest of my life thinking about what a loser I was.

And then I heard, "Psst!"

I turned around, and at the end of Henry's walk, that girl who had been taking tickets at the church stood. She was dressed in a yellow raincoat and pink, polka-dotted rain boots.

"'Ere," she said, gesturing at me to come to her. Not having anything to lose at this point, I picked up my bags in my blistered hands and dragged myself down to the end of the walk where she stood. She looked me up and down and remarked, "You look like you've had a long day. Come and have a pint?"

Normally I think I would have said no, but – like I said – I had nothing to lose. So, like the sad-sack I was, I slowly nodded and followed her down the lane, dragging my suitcases through the mud behind me.

"I'm Gladys Gray," she said, after a few moments of our walking in silence. "What's your name?"

"Matt Evans," I replied.

"You're an American, aren't you?" Apparently it was a rhetorical question, as she immediately went on, "Are you looking for someplace to stay?"

It occurred to me suddenly that I hadn't planned this trip very well. I hadn't booked a hotel room or anything, simply assuming that Henry would welcome me with open arms once he had laid eyes on me.

"I guess I am," I said, slowly, "at least for tonight."

We turned onto a narrow, twisting, tree-lined road, which brought us to the town square – and back to The White Stag. Gladys led me in and we walked up to the bar, she ordering a pint of lager (she was older than she looked). I ordered a Guinness. I don't care for Guinness much – I'm not a big one on dark beers – but it was the only type of British beer that I could name off-hand, and I didn't want to make one of those "Oh, I don't know what I want, what do you have?" kind of scenes. I also ordered some fries -- and happily, the barkeep knew what I meant even though I used the American word for it.

The barkeep planted our drinks in front of us and then went off to get the fries. We sat in silence for a few minutes, sipping our thick, dark, beers, and then Gladys turned to me.

"Look, 'ere," she said, looking up at me with a serious look on her little face. "You don't have to play games with me. I know what your secret is."

My breath caught in my throat. "You *do?*"

"Of course. I could tell it from the moment I laid eyes on you." She narrowed her eyes, examining my face intently. "You're an *actor.*"

I did a confused double take, and then repeated, "An actor?"

"Yeah, I knew it from the start. You don't have to give me that 'oh, I'm a relative' guff what you gave Henry – I figured you gave him that just to lay him off the scent. You're an actor and you come here because you heard about the company and want to join."

"Uh…"

"I figured some actors would turn up here eventually once we begun to make a name for ourselves," she said, nodding with satisfaction. "What shows you done?"

"Well," I said, hesitantly, "I honestly haven't done a whole lot of acting…"

She shrugged. "That's okay. He prefers beginners sometimes -- says they ain't had a chance to learn bad habits. Look here," she said, leaning towards me, "we got a big meeting tomorrow about noon. You come with me, and I'll see that you get in and get a part in the show. Yeh, yeh, Henry gets the final casting choice, but I'm the one what types up the cast sheet – if you ain't on there when he give it to me, I'll make sure you on there before I'm done typin'. You'll prolly just be in the back somewheres, but you'll definitely be in the show. 'Kay?"

She stuck out her hand.

A play.

I had never, ever, ever wanted to be in a play.

I get stage fright alone in the shower.

But what was my alternative plan for this trip? Nothing! Henry had refused to talk to me! So I had a choice between getting involved with this show (and getting a chance to observe my father and get to know him, albeit in a sort of stalker-ish fashion), or going home empty handed and fatherless.

"Okay," I said, taking her small hand in mine and shaking it soundly. It was a decent plan - and yet, somehow I had a feeling that I would regret this.

* * *

I didn't sleep very well that night. I tossed and turned, and finally awoke completely sometime around six. I rolled over and glanced out the window, and saw that the sun wasn't even up yet; the sky was just beginning to be streaked with the pinks and oranges of early morning. I moaned and covered my head with my pillow, but it didn't help. Hopelessly wide-awake, I couldn't coax myself back to sleep. Finally I just sat up in bed and allowed myself to be miserable.

What do you think you're doing, Matt Evans?

This is going to be a disaster. You know it is...

I got out my laptop and tried to email Patty a progress report. Perhaps not surprisingly, the White Stag's spare room did not have Wi-Fi access. Instead I sent her a text message on my phone:

Found HDK already.
Did not tell him.
Waiting for right moment.
Hi to Frank.

The right moment. Would the right moment come? I waited for a reply until I remembered that it was the middle of the night in Chicago. Pat was doubtlessly sound asleep, probably on the couch next to Frank, the both of them dozed off in front of a movie. The phone would beep, she would wake up, check to see who had texted her, swear when she saw it was just me, and go back to sleep instantly.

I got out of bed at seven and went downstairs, where old Jenks' plump, red-cheeked wife gave me a very hearty breakfast of eggs, sausages, thick, greasy slabs of fried bread, and some kind of porridge.

I asked Mrs. Jenks if there was a public computer in town that I could use. She said the library had one, but the library wouldn't be open until later in the day.

So, for lack of anything better to do, I went back up to my room and sat in bed in my shorts, watching a Buster Keaton movie and playing video pinball on my laptop until noon rolled around.

God, I don't want to be in a play.

This thought kept rattling around my head as I dressed. With an incredible sense of impending doom, I dressed wandered down the creaking staircase to the main part of the White Stag. When I stepped off the final step, I found myself an object of instant scrutiny – Gladys and several of the other people from the pantomime the day before were already sitting there at a large table in the center of the room.

Gladys noticed me and waved me over to the table. Putting down the drink she was sipping, she gestured at me to the crowd. "Matt, I want you to meet Mr. Trevor Wilburforce Smythe, Sophia Bainbridge, Dora and Nora Losser, and Daniel Starkey – collectively, the Mosstone Players. Everybody, this is Matthew Evans. He's auditioning."

Mr. Wilburforce Smythe, the tall, distinguished looking older man who had played the king the day before, gave me a curt nod and looked away.

Next in line, Sophia Bainbridge was a very stringy, stern looking middle-aged woman with unnaturally black hair, cut in a rigid bob at her jaw line.

"My name is Sophia," she said, unnecessarily, offering me a cold hand.

"Yes," was all I could think to reply.

Nora and Dora were a pair of blond twin teenage girls, who just giggled at me, then went back to filing their nails in unison. They stared at me unblinkingly, like a pair of creepy Victorian clockwork dolls.

Finally, my eyes came to Daniel, the spotty, teenage boy. He was what I think of as a British man – tall, skinny, big-nosed, small-chinned. I know what it is like to be a teenage boy, so I figured he was my most likely ally in the group.

"Hi, Dan," I said, warmly.

"It's *Daniel*," he snapped. He regarded me with the clearest dislike of the bunch.

"Well, that's enough for introductions," Gladys said hastily. "Would you like to tell us something about yourself, Matt?"

That was probably the last thing I would like, but since, as a whole, the Mosstone Players offered me a glare of open hostility – I figured I ought to say something. "Well, uh, I'm an American... first time in England... Doing some family research... Thought I would – see what this theater thing is all about." I cleared my throat. "That's about it."

The group stared at me.

I sipped my thick, bitter beer.

"So," I said, attempting to be friendly again. "Putting on a show, eh?"

No response whatsoever. Sophia turned her face away, the twins closely examined their cuticles, and the two other men at the table sipped their own beers and regarded me with suspicion.

"Uh," I said, feeling that I ought to go on, "just so you know – I don't really want to be *in* the show. I just thought I'd observe – be a back stage hand, or something."

The group at the table underwent an instantaneous change. Suddenly they were all smiles – even Daniel Starkey, who seconds before seemed to be having difficulty restraining himself from spitting at me. Now he was giving me a wide grin, exposing a prominent over-bite.

"Well, that is exactly what we need, Matthew," Sophia said huskily. "I've been telling Henry for ages that having the actors handling their own costumes, props and so on – it's just not professional."

"Strictly speaking we're *not* professional," Mr. Smythe remarked, sipping his own beer. He eyed me quizzically. "What made you interested in the Theatre, Matthew? I became interested when I was a mere lad of fifteen. Of course, that was the sixties and I thought I'd be a television actor because that was the new thing, you know, television –"

"Of course we're *technically* not professional," Sophia interrupted him, ignoring me, "but that's not the point. No one will respect us as actors if we don't put our foot down and say, 'I am an actor, not a stagehand. I do not carry my own props.' Don't you think so, Matthew?"

"Where you from in America?" Daniel said, excited. "New York? I know this guy from school called Mark Evans – you his cousin or something?"

The sudden kindness of the group was as scary their hatred – I didn't like the attention and wanted to leave. But Gladys smiled at me, encouragingly. Something about her warmed me to the crowd. I was about to try and answer the various questions I had been asked when I was saved abruptly –

The doors of the pub burst open and there stood Henry Dale Kitteridge in a dazzle of sunlight. He was dressed in a shoulder cape, hat, and walking stick; he even had gray spats that matched his suit, and gray, leather half-gloves. He looked something like my idea of a theatrical impresario of the early nineteen-hundreds.

The group sitting around me broke into enthusiastic applause. Henry floated into the room, chin in the air.

"Hurrah for the director!" Daniel cried, his voice squeaking.

"Oh, please, please, that's not necessary," Henry said, clearly enjoying every moment of it. The applause continued until Henry took his place at the table – which he did by throwing down his hat and cane in the chair and then pacing around the table at a frenetic speed.

"Gladys, to work!" he cried as he ran past her. "We haven't a moment to lose."

Gladys leapt to her feet with a notebook in hand and followed behind him, taking notes as he spoke.

He fiddled his gloves nervously as he walked, pressing the index finger of his right hand between each of his other fingers.

"As you know," he sang out as he circled the table, "the Mosstone Players turned five years old yesterday. We have had a successful run in this town from a critical standpoint: however, our last three shows did not turn a profit. And if our production of *Princess and the Pea* did not turn a profit, we would not have the funds to do another performance."

He paused momentously, ceasing his frantic pacing long enough to settle a hand on Daniel's shoulder and one on Mr. Smythe's. "We did *not* earn a profit."

There was a gasp from Sophia and she covered her mouth with her hand. A silent cloud of doom visibly settled upon them all. I felt guilty that I wasn't particularly affected by the news, and tried to look suitably mournful.

Finally, after letting it sink in, Henry went on, "But all is not lost. I may have found – a sponsor."

A cheer went up from the group, but Henry interrupted the joy of his actors with a strident cry of, "Wait!"

Everyone froze, and all eyes were on him – a situation he seemed to luxuriate in. Obviously playing the crowd, he announced in Shakespearian voice, "We are not out of the woods, my children. Before Lord Hatfield agrees to sponsor us permanently, we must put on a play of his choice and perform it well – damn well. *And* we have to turn a profit. We have exactly three weeks to throw this miracle together."

He leaned over the table, knuckles down, looking from face to face. "We must succeed! For the sake of this company, for the sake of theatre, for the sake of this town! Are you with me?"

"Hurrah!" the unanimous cry went up.

"Then we cannot be stopped! Get your scripts from Gladys tomorrow morning for rehearsal tomorrow night. God be with you, my friends!"

His actors instantly dispersed, leaving just Henry and Gladys, who looked exhausted. Henry turned to her, and in an un-theatrical, mild tone of voice remarked, "You're the light of my life, Gladys. Could you possibly have those copies of the script ready for them to pick up tomorrow, dear one? Thanks ever so much."

He wrapped his arms around her and held her for a long moment – a bit too long in my opinion – then turned to pick up his hat and cane, at which point he finally noticed me. He snapped, "Who the hell are you?"

I sat there, startled, not sure what to say.

"Henry," Gladys said quietly, tugging at his sleeve, "this young man wants to be an actor."

"Oh, he *does*, does he?" Henry narrowed his eyes at me. "So you want to be an *actor*, do you?"

I didn't know what to say to that either, so I just sat there stupidly as Henry slowly paced towards me. He stopped in front of my chair and put one gloved hand on the table in front of me.

"Well, sonny," he said, affecting kindliness, "why do you want to be an actor?"

I stammered. "I – I…"

"Too slow!" he bellowed, smacking the table fiercely. "Look, here, young man: if you're here because you've 'got something to say,' or because you want to work out the emotional problems you got from your parents' divorce, I would advise you to take your aspiration and locate it where the sun doth not shine. That kind of 'acting', if it can be dignified with such a term, is nothing more than public masturbation. Do you *want* to masturbate in public?"

"Uh –"

"Look," he said, taking my face in his gloved hands and looking deep into my eyes. "There is only *one* reason to be an actor. Do you know what that is?" He paused momentously, then released my face and raised his hands in the air. "To entertain!!   That is the *cardinal rule* of my theatre company!   We are here to entertain an audience *and for no other reason*. Do you understand?"

"Yes," I said, faintly.

"Good!   You can be an understudy. Gladys, get this young man a script."

And with that, he scooped up his cape, hat and cane, and was gone.

"See?" Gladys said with a smile. "It ain't that hard to become an actor."

CHAPTER THREE

The Right Moment

I was awakened at one-thirty in the morning by an urgent beeping from my cell phone.

The text message read:

Right moment yet?   :-P

Irritably, I started to text Patty back – but kept hitting the wrong buttons and finally just threw my phone down on the blankets.

I should never have used that term. Pat liked to torment me with the fact that I had told her, in a weak moment, that I was waiting for "the right moment" to ask her to marry me. Well, of course, the moment never came, and Pat broke up with me and found herself a rich, charming, podgy surgeon to marry.

Don't get me wrong: Frank's a really great guy. *I* would have chosen him over me. But that phrase "the right moment" continues to haunt me – although, in point of fact, I didn't miss the chance with Pat because I was waiting for the right moment.

That was part of it, but when you get right down to it, I missed the chance because I was scared.

* * *

Gladys lived in one of a group of identical and very snugly spaced white bungalows near the square. At nine o'clock that morning, I knocked on her door.

You're an idiot, I thought to myself as my knuckles rapped against the wood. Why are you doing this? Just tell him that you're his son and get it over with, and you'll save yourself a heck of a lot of trouble.

The door jerked open and Gladys appeared in the doorway in an over-sized sweatshirt and leggings – her eyes popped open wide at the sight of me and a huge smile split her face.

"Matthew!" she cried, grabbing my arm and dragging me into the cozy little living room. "Come in and meet me Mum!"

Gladys's Mum was in the kitchen eating cereal. She was a chubby, white-haired Gladys in a bathrobe. She looked up at me in horror and shielded her face – then reached down and tried to pull her bathrobe shut. "Gladys! I ain't decent!"

"Oh, Mum, it's all right," she said, shoving me towards the lady. "Matthew, this is my Mum, Doris Gray. My Dad ain't home. Mum – Matthew's the new actor in Henry's group. He's an American."

"Nice to meet you, Matchew – *now get him out!*"

I was bustled back to the door and Mrs. Gray slammed it in my face. A moment later, Gladys re-opened it with my copy of the script in her hand.

"Here," she said, apologetically. "Sorry about that. Mum hates for people to see her before she got makeup on. Where are you going now?"

"Just back to my room, I guess."

"Well, hang on then – I'm off to work. Let me get me scarf and I'll walk with you."

She ducked back into the house for a moment.

I looked down at the script in my hand and read the title – *Macbeth*.

My stomach did a flip-flop.

Insanity – just insanity.

Understudy? Wasn't that, like, where you memorized everyone else's lines in case somebody was injured? Well, what if somebody *was* injured? I couldn't just jump up and perform on a moment's notice – I didn't even know if I could perform on a year's notice.

I can't do it! I can't!

Gladys reappeared, pulling a red hat down over her head as she tugged the door shut behind her. "All right!   Let's go!"

"You know, Gladys," I said, hastily, "I really think I need to go over and talk to Henry about this. I'll see you later, okay?"

"Oh." Her face was blank for a moment, and then she smiled, shrugging her shoulders. "Okay. That's fine. See you tonight, then."

I had to get this thing with Henry settled. I had to tell him that I couldn't do this understudy thing, and come clean about the real reason that I was here.   I marched out of Gladys' yard, out of town, and out to the little cottage in the cow pasture where Henry lived. As I was walking, I rehearsed what I was going to say.

"Look, Henry..." I cleared my throat. "Mr. Kitteridge, I can't do this. I didn't come to Mosstone to be an actor. I came here to find you because I believe I might be... your son."

It sounded horribly dramatic and soap-operatic. A cow listened to me with bland indifference as I passed.

When I neared Henry's bungalow, I noticed something odd; a very, very nice car was parked in the road in front of the house – a 1964 Aston Martin, a freakin' *James Bond* car. As I passed through Henry's front gate, a black-suited old man with a monocle exited Henry's front door, followed by Henry – who took one look at me and threw his hands in the air.

"Matthew!" he cried. "My son!"

He ran over to me, embracing me fondly and then kissing me on both cheeks. Completely disoriented I stood there, mute and frozen.

"Lord Hatfield," Henry cried, throwing his arm around my shoulders and dragging me over to the well-dressed gentleman, "this is that young man I was telling you about – Matthew Hatfield-Evans; a fine, upstanding young man."

"Charmed," Lord Hatfield said, inclining his head to me ever so slightly. "Hatfield-Evans, eh? Perhaps you're an American cousin!"

"But my name's not…" I started, and was instantly interrupted.

"Matthew is the visiting artist I was discussing with you," Henry said, digging his fingernails into my shoulder. "Just arrived from America, where he recently finished a brilliant off-Broadway stint in August Wilson's *Fences.* Are you familiar with the play?"

"I can't say I am," Lord Hatfield said, adjusting his monocle at me.

I found my voice enough to gulp, "*I did not!*"

"He means he wasn't brilliant. What modesty!" Henry said, punching me in the chest with apparent jocularity. He began shoving me towards the door of his house. "Now, Matthew – if you'd just step inside, we can discuss your character's motivation in a few moments. Au revoir, Lord Hatfield! T.T.F.N.!"

He kicked me smartly in the pants and shoved me through the open door – then leapt in behind me and slammed it.

"*'Struth!*" he cried, grabbing the handkerchief out of his front pocket and daubing his forehead with it. "I'm glad *that's* over with!"

I was staring at him open-mouthed.

"You – you lied!" I gasped.

Henry crossed the room, stopping at the fireplace, where he picked up a pack of cigarettes and immediately began smoking. He ignored me vehemently.

"You just lied to that man!" I said, violently pointing at the door. "How could you do that?"

"Oh, come now," Henry said, waving a cigaretted hand at me dismissively. "It wasn't lying, really. It was just creative truth. After all – as far as I know, you haven't *not* done an off-Broadway production of *Fences*. Have you?"

"No! Wait – what?"

"Well, there, you see? Now I know! I won't go saying that again. Look," he said, walking over to me and squeezing my injured shoulder, "Lord Hatfield came here in an obstreperous mood and I needed something to sweeten the deal. Telling him I had a 'visiting artist from America' was just what it took! And look," he added, gesturing to the coffee table, on which lay a check.

"He's paid, up-front, for the entire production!"

"Mr. Kitteridge," I said, trying to keep my voice low. "My middle name isn't Hatfield, it's Hen –"

"Well, it's better than your real name – whatever it was. Hatfield-Evans can be your stage name."

"Mr. Kitteridge!" I said, desperately. "I came here today to tell you that I can't do this play and that I –"

"Matthew *Hatfield*," Henry said, aghast, "don't even say such a thing."

"But I can't! I'm no actor, but I am your –!"

"Look at me – look!" Henry commanded suddenly, throwing his cigarette heedlessly aside. "Do you know what you see before you?"

Suddenly Henry's face was tired – his shoulders bowed – his chest sunken. He staggered backwards to an armchair and sank into it wearily, bowing his head.

"Matthew, you see before you a broken man. Theatre is a heartless whore that sucks your life away and breaks your soul and gives you nothing – *nothing!* – in return. What do I have to show for thirty years in the business? Do I have legions of adoring fans? No. Do I have a pension? No. Do I have a wife and children to look after me in my dotage?"

He smiled, shaking his head slowly. "If *only* I were so *lucky.* No, no – Theatre has been my wife and vagabond children, who beat me and starve me and then leave me to fend for myself in the rain. And yet I keep going back – always I go back."

My mouth hung open. After a moment I finally managed to stammer, "If it's so bad – why do you keep doing it?"

"Because it's all I know how to do." He looked up at me, and his eyes were wet – gleaming. "Matthew... please. I'm out of money, and I'm out of time. Unless Lord Hatfield agrees to become our permanent sponsor... I don't know what I'm going to do. This company is all I have, and if I lose it... Oh God!" He dragged his hand across his face raggedly. "Please – *please* help me! *Please* do the show! Swear to me that you'll do it!"

I couldn't help but slowly nod my head.

"Perfect!" Henry cried, leaping to his feet and embracing me violently. "Now I've got some phone calls to make, so run off and be a good lad. I'll see you at rehearsal."

Before I quite realized what was going on, he had backed me out the door and slammed it in my face.

* * *

"You're *what?*" Patty said over the phone, her voice aghast.

"I'm just an understudy," I said hastily, leaning against the bed frame. "That means I probably won't even go on – I'm just there in case somebody can't go on, and I'm told that's pretty unlikely."

"But what if somebody *can't* go on?"

I swallowed. The cell phone felt kind of hot against my ear. I looked down and ran a finger through my chest hair. I spun a lump of it around my finger for a moment, until it tangled and hurt.

"Well... I... I guess I would..."

"Exactly," Patty said harshly. "You have no idea what you're doing. You need to just tell this man that you're his son and get the damn thing over with! You hang on a minute and I'm going to have Frank talk some sense to you. Frank – Frank, come here, and talk some sense to Matt. Matt? Frank's coming."

I didn't want to talk to Frank, since he would just repeat what Patty had said. I hastily lied that I had to go and clicked the phone shut.

I was on the verge of throwing it across the room when there was a knock at the door -- I looked up and discovered that the door was open. Sophia stood there, leaning against the doorframe, staring at me with an odd little gleam in her steely gray eye.

You know the "Dragon Lady" in the old *Terry and the Pirates* comic strip? Or the Spider Woman in *Kiss of the Spider Woman*? Imagine one of them – forty years older, with dyed hair, unflattering, overly-youthful clothes and leathery skin.

I suddenly wished I was wearing a shirt.

"Sorry for the interruption," Sophia said, slithering into the room and standing against the doorframe. "Was that your lady friend in America?"

"Yes," I said hastily, jumping off my bed. Technically, it was true: Patty is both a lady and a friend. I snatched up a shirt and buttoned it over my chest at super speed. "Is rehearsal starting? We better go down."

I hustled Sophia out of my room and locked it securely behind me. I felt beads of cold sweat on my lower back.

When we reached the pub, the Mosstone Players were scattered across the room. Gladys and the girls were whispering over the table, while Trevor Wilberforce Smythe and Daniel played darts. Those two greeted me with a cold eye.

I hastily abandoned Sophia and took a seat next to Gladys, who seemed to ignore me for a few moments before turning and giving me one of her characteristic smiles, and pushing a Guinness across the table towards me. I was getting tired of dark beers – but with her buying them for me, it seemed impolite to say so. I sipped at it, getting a mouthful of tangy, musty bitterness for my trouble. It's like drinking a basement.

Gladys went back to whispering at the girls, and I looked over at Mr. Smythe and Daniel. Perhaps I ought to make an attempt to get on the good side of my fellow actors (and get away from Sophia, who had seated herself uncomfortably close to me). I got up and walked over to them.

"Darts, eh?" I said jocularly, sipping my beer.

"You seem to enjoy stating the obvious," Mr. Smythe said.

I took another sip, ignoring his attitude, then asked gently, "May I play?"

"'Sa free country," Daniel said, gazing at me through slitted eyes. He put a handful of darts in my hand and stood back.

I weighed a dart in my hand. They were cheap things, some missing a wing here and there, and the board before me was badly pockmarked and chipped.

Okay. Not to brag – but shooting darts is the one thing in life that I know I'm good at. Setting my beer on a nearby table, I took careful aim – and in a few seconds, had all five darts sticking amicably out of the black center circle.

Daniel's mouth dropped open. "Cor!!"

Trevor Wilberforce Smythe was a bit more reserved in his praise – but he was clearly impressed as well. He took a long drink of his own beer and then said, quietly, "Not bad."

"I did tournaments in college," I explained, walking over to the board and retrieving the darts for Daniel. "I flunked Algebra twice because I was spending so much time playing. It was worth it, though: I've played darts many times since then, but I haven't used Algebra once."

"Well," Mr. Smythe said, in measured tones, "if you understudy as well as you play darts, Daniel and I need not fear missing a performance."

They were warming to me. Putting a smile on my face, I cheerfully asked, "Who did you guys get cast as?"

"Daniel is MacDuff," Mr. Smythe said, "and I am the Scotsman himself."

"The who?" I said, and then snapped my fingers. "Oh, you mean Macb --"

"Don't!" Daniel cried, a panicked look on his face.

I froze, confused.

"Do not," Smythe said coldly, "*ever* say the name of the Scottish play."

"It's terrible bad luck," Daniel explained.

"Oh," I said, slowly. "I gotcha." I think I might have heard of that theatrical superstition before, but I didn't think that people really believed in it. While Daniel took his shots at the dartboard, I wondered how they were going to do the show without ever saying Macbeth's name. Perhaps it doesn't count when it's in the script.

Henry burst into the pub as he had the day before – only this time haloed in the orange light of the dying sun. "Actors, *to work!*"

The Mosstone Players instantly dropped what they were doing and returned to their seats at the table, all eyes focused on Henry. This time, rather than pacing the table, he walked up and delicately seated himself at the head of the table, shrugging his cape off into the chair behind him.

"All right," he said, deliberately. "You all picked up scripts with your names and your characters' names earlier today, correct? I had Sophia as Lady M, Trevor as M, Daniel as Macduff – and myself, Nora and Dora as everyone else. Well, since that time I have evaluated my choices and decided to make a few changes since we have young Matthew here as well." He paused and glanced at a notebook in his hand. "Daniel – Banquo. Trevor – Duncan and Macduff. Matthew – you will star."

For a moment I didn't understand. And then my stomach clenched in stark horror.

Smythe and Daniel immediately began to protest. Smythe shouted that this was an outrage and Daniel complained that he'd already marked all his lines in the script -- but Henry silenced them with a hand.

"But," I gulped, "I don't want to be Mac --"

"*Don't!!*" Henry shrieked, wild-eyed. The cast looked at me in horror. "Don't you dare, don't you *dare* say the name of the Scottish play!"

"Did you hear what the lad said, Kitteridge?" Smythe said, banging his fist on the table. "He doesn't want to be the lead!"

"He's just being modest," Henry said, flicking a wrist. "The young man is star material. Perhaps his stage name should be Matthew Starr."

"You said *my* stage name should be Starr," Daniel squeaked.

"Oh, did I?" Henry frowned. "Well, that's no good – it'll look like nepotism. How about Daniel... Dur...frin...son? I always thought that would be a fine name for a young man of your, um, type."

"Henry," I said, urgently, beads of sweat rolling down my forehead as I felt Daniel and Smythe's eyes shoot daggers at me. I got up, walked around the table to where he sat and took hold of his arm, and lead him into a dark corner of the room. *"Why?"*

"Oh, didn't I mention earlier?" He gazed at me innocently. "After I told Lord Hatfield about our visiting artist, he decided it would be a waste of your talents for you to be an understudy. He made it a condition of this probationary sponsorship that you play the lead."

"But I can't!" I hissed, twisting my script in my hands. "I'm not an actor!"

"Matthew," he said, taking my shoulders in his hands and looking into my eyes again, "I'm sorry I didn't tell you earlier – it was a genuine mistake. I was flustered. I know you didn't know about this when you swore to help me… so, if finding this out you would rather not do the show – I release you. Forget your promise to me. *Renege.* I'll just go to Lord Hatfield and tell him I can't do the show, I'll return the scripts if I can, and…" His eyes misted up slightly. "Oh, I'll get by. Somehow. Granted a chance like this to salvage a bloke's career doesn't come up more than once, but – who knows? Maybe I can get a job sweeping up here at the pub. It would be poetic justice in a way…"

Oh God. I couldn't be responsible for ruining my father's career. I sighed deeply, covering my eyes with my hands.

"But – Henry, I'm not an actor!"

"Phff! You think any of *them* are actors?" He gestured vaguely at his company members. "The only one with any professional credits is Sophia – who thirty years ago spent a month as a chorus girl in a London musical. You're as qualified as any of them. Back to work."

He grabbed my arm and dragged me back to the table.

"Now, see here, Kitteridge," Smythe began, but Henry interrupted by slamming his hands on the table and upsetting my drink.

"Who is the director?" he cried, looking at them all with a steely eye. "Might I remind you – I am. This is not about ego. This is not about who plays whom. This is about entertaining an audience.

Look at this young man here," he said, pointing at me and causing me intense discomfort. "He's playing the lead, and he's pretending he doesn't even want it! You should be emulating this young man's false modesty!"

My cheeks burned fiercely. I couldn't look them in the eyes.

"Not even to mention that if *I*," Henry went on, "as the director, think that you would be best in a certain role, that is the role you shall have. If you don't want to abide by my rules you can walk out that door right now!"

He pointed at the door violently, then folded his arms and waited. The girls sat mute – they had no stake in the matter. But it took Trevor Smythe a good fifty seconds to get the cords in his neck to stop twitching. Finally he gave a stiff nod and turned his face away.

I tried to get up, but Gladys reached under the table and held me down.

"Good," Henry said at last. "Now, to business – we will have a read-through."

That read-through was one of the most miserable experiences of my life. I whispered Macbeth's lines, hating the sound of my own, untrained voice – knowing that I spoke horribly flat, nothing like an actor. The two men I had so recently been dart-friends with were now visibly shooting darts at me from their eyes. And I couldn't even blame them! If I were one of them, I would have hated me, too!

Henry chain-smoked the whole time, ignoring the proceedings and whispering to Gladys at his side, who dutifully giggled under her breath and took notes. He would occasionally pause to look up and shout, "Louder! More Scottish!"

I couldn't do a Scottish accent to save my life. I shifted between Australian and Transylvania, finally settling on a bad Sean Connery impression. Mind you, this lasted for three, maybe four hours, until the pub was closing up for the night and old Jenks came over to shoo us out.

I tried to apologize to Daniel and Mr. Smythe before they left, but they seemed in a hurry to get away. Henry evaporated into the air, vanishing while my back was turned. Before I knew what was happening only Gladys remained; she sat at the table, making notes on her clipboard. I started to speak to her, but stopped. I felt dirty and ashamed, and didn't want to speak to anyone.

I turned away and ducked into the stairwell, running back to my room without a goodnight. I heard a soft tap on my door a while later and I thought, maybe, she had come up to say goodbye — but I was too humiliated by this situation to discuss matters.

I turned out the light and pretended I was asleep, and eventually I heard footsteps pad away down the hall.

CHAPTER FOUR

The Worst Experience of My Life, Part I

Despite the impression you might have gotten about me up until this point, I'm really an organized person.

Rolling over in bed and looking at the copy of *Macbeth* on my nightstand, I realized I was getting nowhere fast towards any of the goals I'd had when I set out on this trip – I was terribly sidetracked. And it's not like I had forever: I had accumulated a month of vacation at my tech support job and it seemed I would be using all of it. After that, I would be out of money *and* out of time.

So I purchased a notebook from the store and borrowed a ballpoint pen from the pub, and sat down on my bed and made a nice, organized, list of things I wanted to learn from this trip.

Kitteridge History: Family Origins, Birth, Career

Henry and Mom: How did they meet? Why did they break up?

Does Henry have any genetic conditions I should know about?

Did Henry Know About Me? If So, Why No Contact?

Similarities between Henry and myself?

I sucked on my front teeth for a minute, considering how many of these points I could currently answer.

I crossed out the word Career, and then sat back and looked at my list with dissatisfaction. Strictly speaking I could answer that final point as well: Henry and I were nothing alike. He was manipulative and flamboyant. I was forthright and timid. We couldn't have been less alike if we tried. Inverse opposites.

I suppose I could probably answer the forth point as well; it seemed highly unlikely that Henry knew about my existence. He had said my name... Yet there wasn't one of those moments like, *"Your name is Matthew Henry Evans? Say, was your mother's name Josephine Johnson Evans? And were you born about thirty-one years ago...? Oh my god!!"*

Nope. He had been told my name, and there was not a glimmer of recognition. I got up and stared out my window at a rooftop below. What if I was the result of a one-night stand? That didn't sound like Mom, but I would not be shocked at Henry. And if that were the case, he might not even remember my mother. But if it *had* been a one-night stand, why had he given her his real name? That didn't seem to jive with his personality... it seemed unusually *honest*. For that matter, it seemed unusually... *dishonest*... of my mother not to mention my existence to Henry. Then all at once, something really terrible occurred to me.

What if Henry wasn't my father?

In the last stages of the cancer, Mom had been fairly out-of-it. Not in any pain, but the medication she was on made her incoherent and confused. What if... what if, in her confusion, she wrote down the name of the wrong man? Perhaps she heard about Henry somewhere, or maybe she saw him in a show – or read about him somewhere. I mean she didn't give me any real information about him. She didn't even really give me his address – just his hometown, the sort of thing you might find in a show program in an actor's bio. She could just as easily have written down "Harrison Ford, Hollywood" – and being the chump I am, I wouldn't have questioned it.

What if I had come all this way and gotten involved with this ridiculous show for nothing?

* * *

The next rehearsal was to be held at Henry's house. I was glad, because this would give me a chance to learn more about him and look for clues – photographs, keepsakes – anything that might indicate that he'd once had a relationship with my mother. A framed photo of them together with the inscription "To the Fellow Parent of My Child" would be nice.

I arrived at his front gate at the same time as Gladys, who, to my surprise, seemed to be trying to ignore me as we walked down Henry's front path together. She flatly disregarded my greeting, but by the time we reached Henry's front gate I saw her glance at me out of the corner of her eye.

"That's a relief," I remarked lightly. "I was beginning to think I was invisible."

She cracked a half-smile and looked away. We waited for Henry to answer his bell in silence. I figured she was just in a bad mood. Women do have mysterious bad moods sometimes. Although... well, what little I knew of her, it didn't seem like her to act like this. After a few moments, growing uncomfortable, I asked, "Say, Gladys – you're not upset at me, are you?"

"Upset?" she repeated, looking at me out of the corner of her eye. "I have no reason whatsoever to be upset at you."

"Well, that's a relief!" I said. Only later did it occur to me that she hadn't said that she *wasn't* upset.

At last, the door swung open – and there was Henry in a bright red Kimono, bowl of Twiglets in one and a cigarette in the other. The Abba song *Dancing Queen* was blaring in the background and a gust of warm, smoky air hit me in the face.

"My children!" he cried, exultantly. "Come in, come in – you can help me get the furniture moved. We're going to start blocking tonight."

I didn't know what blocking was – but I went in and helped Gladys move Henry's living room furniture to his hallway.

By the time we were done the rest of the cast had arrived; playing host, Henry offered everyone a Twiglet and then made us sit on cushions in the center of his living room floor with our scripts. He asked Gladys to turn down the Abba that still blared out of an ancient record player in the corner, and then jumped up onto the couch that jutted out of the hallway.

"Now, children," he said, standing on his couch in a Napoleonic pose, "as you may have noticed from the number of characters I was performing during the read-through, there are far, far too many people in this play for a company of our size. So, I've made a few cuts." He whipped out his copy of the script and began, "Turn to page four – cross out everything form 'What bloody man is that?' to 'Go get him surgeons'."

We spent about the next hour like that, crossing out long sections of dialogue in our scripts. At the finish of it, Mr. Smythe looked up with displeasure and announced, "There isn't much left of the original play."

"Ho-hum," Henry said, yawning and settling back on his couch with cigarette in hand. "Your average audience would be bored stiff if we did the play as-is. And might I remind you, we have a lot of very average audiences in this town."

"I must protest," Smythe said. "Isn't it a trifle presumptuous of us to simply butcher William Shakespeare to fit our own ends?"

"We'll leave the unabridged version for Branagh." Henry snapped his fingers. "Gladys, come sit next to me. We shall start from the beginning from the three witches – Dora, Nora, Sophia, and after that Nora and Dora can go home because we'll only need the others for the rest of the evening."

We ran through the blocking of that first part – where the

Scotsman comes in and meets the witches and is told that he'll be King and whatnot – with Henry stopping us every other line to give us an instruction. Turn this way, walk three steps to the right and look over your shoulder, etcetera. The whole process made me relax: the sheer mechanical quality of blocking made sense to me. Say a line, turn right. Say a line, step back. Say a line, cross in front. *That* sort of thing I can handle.

It got so automatic that I was able to start focusing my attention on other things. When other people were saying their lines, I was able to look around Henry's house.

His walls were lined with posters from plays that he had done – *King Lear, Equus, Look Back in Anger,* some with dates for performances as far back as 1972. It was like a rogue's gallery of Henry's career. Most of them were with small companies with names like "The Darrowby Township Players" – but there were a few from London, and even one Royal Shakespeare Company. Closest to the door were his most recent productions – a slew of goofy looking pantomimes. *Princess and the Pea. Jack and the Beanstalk. Cinderella.*

My eyes drifted across the wall to a small, faded poster in the corner near where I was standing. It had a black-and-white representation of a very young looking Henry's face, over which was proclaimed,

---

1976 World Tour!

Held over in Chicago for Three More Weeks!

The Royal Oxbridge Society of London Presents –

HAMLET

Starring **Henry Dale Kitteridge.**

Tickets available August 26th.

He was in Chicago in August 1976??!

August 1976 was eight months before I would be born – in Northwestern Hospital, Chicago, Illinois.

For a moment my heart rate went out of control, but then I forced myself to calm down and look at the facts. Okay: this did *not* prove that Henry was my father – or even that he and mother had ever met each other. It simply proved that he was in Chicago for several months around the point I was… assembled. It was suspicious, but it didn't rule out my mother being confused in her last days and naming a casual acquaintance – or possibly even a performer who she saw on stage – as my Dad.

As I stared at the poster and debated these facts, I became aware that someone was talking. Out of nowhere Henry clapped his hands in front of my face.

"Wake up, flippetygibbert! This is no time for gawking and daydreaming."

"Sorry," I gulped.

"We're moving on now to the scene where Lady Macca convinces you to kill Duncan. Now, stand *here*," he added, dragging me across the room, "next to this cushion, which we'll say is a battlement you're standing behind, and we'll get started! Sophia, go stand in the doorway and you start from there."

Oh god. I'd forgotten that the Dragon Lady was playing my *wife*.

Sophia slinked over to the doorway – then slinked into the center of the room and read her little soliloquy, gyrating her hips the whole time. (I am relatively certain that Shakespeare did not intend that.) My lower back sweated beads of ice. Then came my big entrance with the line, "My dearest love, Duncan comes here tonight."

Henry interrupted my walking and speaking with a sharp cry. "No, no – say the line *after* you reach her. And when you reach her, throw your arms around her. She's your wife, for God's sake. You've been away and this is the first time you've seen her in days.

Come on, dammit – make me *feel* it."

Now my hands were sweating too. "I thought this was just blocking."

"I'll block you in the head if you question me again. Positions!"

I walked back over to my cushion, then Sophia said my cue with gyrating hips and I approached her, threw my arms around her and said, in a shaky voice, "My dearest love, Duncan comes here tonight."

"Now," Henry interrupted, jumping off the couch and approaching us, "Soph, after he says that, kiss him and lay your head upon his neck, then when you speak again, lift your face up. Let's see some passion, people."

This was getting worse and worse.

We had to repeat that bit about ten times for some reason – each time Sophia getting a bit more aggressive with me. I try not to judge people's physical appearances; after all, we *all* get old someday.

But she was appallingly unattractive.

Up close her skin had kind of a strange, wrinkly-but-stretched appearance, and when she kissed me she tasted like a combination of cigarettes, baked beans and menthol. By the time we got to the part where she goes off to check on Duncan, I had been indecently groped and chewed on all in the name of Theatre. And I have NEVER been so relieved as when Henry let us move on to the next bit.

Henry had me pace back and forth as I said it, as if I was thinking out loud. I began, "If it were done when 'tis done, then 'twere well…" and ended, something like twenty minutes later, with, "… but vaulting ambition, which o'er leaps itself, and falls on th'other."

"Fine," Henry said, waving his hand dismissively. "Let's go on. Sophia – get back up there."

"Wait a second," I interrupted, "don't you want me to repeat that bit? I have no idea what that entire speech was about."

Henry narrowed his eyes at me. "We are working on *blocking* today, Matthew. We will work on *emoting* later."

"I know, I know - but isn't that a problem? I mean, I don't know how I should be saying any of this. It's like gibberish!"

"Blocking!" Henry snapped. "Sophia – enter stage right!"

And then she was all over me again.

The rest of the evening for me was an exhausting blur of being alternately yelled at and humped. I felt tired, humiliated and dirty – I just wanted to go back to my room at the pub, take a long, hot, sterile shower, and go to sleep. At last, Henry said that the boys and Sophia could go home.

I staggered to the hallway and reached for my jacket, but Henry said, "Where do you think you're going?"

"I'm a boy," I said, confused.

"Oh, so you're a boy, are you? Well, don't they teach *boys* chivalry in America? Are you going to let this poor young thing move all the furniture back into the living room by herself?"

Gladys was, without success, trying to drag the couch back from the hallway to the living room. I sighed deeply and then went to help.

Henry stood and watched, giving "helpful" direction. "No, no – the ottoman goes over there. No, closer to the chair. Closer. How am I supposed to put my feet up on that? I'm not a giant. Closer! Now get that table and put it under the clock. Did I say under the poster? *I said under the clock!*"

When we finally finished, I didn't even say goodnight to him – I was too tired and annoyed. I snatched up my jacket and stormed out his door without a backward glance.

"Matthew!"

I stopped. Gladys stood in the doorway of Henry's house with my script in hand. She held it out to me, a sympathetic smile on her face.

I marched back and took it from her – then flipped through it, sighing. "Gladys... I don't know how much more of this I can take."

"Don't give up," she said, putting a hand on my shoulder in a sisterly way. "This just the first rehearsal. Things change."

"Not the parts that bother me the most."

I looked up at her. She was standing with her back to the light; her face was lost in shadow.

"Gladys, I know nothing about Shakespeare! I don't understand half of what I was saying!"

Sophia materialized out of the night with a cigarette in hand; evidently she had hung around outside to smoke. She stepped in front of Gladys, and in her deep voice she announced, "You're just un-used to the rhythm, darling. You're trying to speak like an American, but you can't do that and get the correct sound out of this language. I'll work with you, if you like," she said, leaning close to me. "Come back to my place. I can teach you the rhythm of Shakespeare."

I may be naïve in certain respects – but not *that* naïve. I politely declined, saying that I had to get up early the next morning.

"Very well," she said, turning away with dignity and gyrating towards the gate. She stopped and turned back momentarily, tapping her cigarette delicately. "But if you change your mind – don't forget. My door is always open to young actors."

"I'm sure that it is," I said, and turned away, shuddering. I was going to say goodnight to Gladys and thank her for giving my script back – but she had quietly closed Henry's door in my face.

CHAPTER FIVE

Homeless

I found that I was sinking lower, lower, and lower – until my nose was touching my lunch. I shook myself, pinched myself, and shoveled a forkful of the tasteless fish into my mouth.

It was Wednesday, lunchtime, and it seemed like I had been here forever – trying to memorize lines, trying to eat, trying not to fall asleep.

Have *you* ever tried to memorize a script? It's like memorizing a whole book, word for word! You've got to know everything that your character says, *and* everything that all the other characters are saying so that you'll know when to say your stuff. I read the script completely from end-to-end at least three times a day, and yet I still could only recite my first few lines -- and I still had only the vaguest idea of what my character was actually saying. (Seriously. The only thing more mysterious to me than why people still perform these plays is why anybody would want to go see one. What kind of person enjoys this crap? Do people just pretend to like it so that they'll seem smart or what?)

Anyway, we were supposed to be "off book" in three more rehearsals and I didn't know how I was going to do it.

That had been the plight of my last few days: the nights, when I slept at all, had been spent plagued with nightmares about walking out on stage – not only without pants, but without *a single line* memorized. The audience began booing, my cast members hated me, and Henry – he usually died. Except for that one dream, where he was a tomato.

"God." I rubbed my eyes. They felt like they were filled with sand, or were on fire, or possibly filled with sand that was on fire. The question I had about Henry preyed on my mind and weren't getting answered. The performance of this play was gut-stompingly soon. And what did I have to look forward to? Tomorrow and tomorrow and tomorrow, creeping in this petty pace from day to day, till last syllable of recorded time…?

Wait, was that from the play?! Did I accidentally memorize something?! I flipped open my script and dumped my cup of coffee on the countertop.

Mrs. Jenks was suddenly in front of me wiping the counter down with a wet cloth. I hastily pretended to be really enjoying my fish and chips. "Sorry about that."

"No trouble. Salt and vinegar, love?" she asked. She proffered me a sticky bottle and a shaker.

"Thanks," I said, taking them. I wasn't a fan of vinegar but it might give the fish some flavor. As I shook a few drops onto my lunch, I lightly asked, "Say, Mrs. Jenks – you've lived in Mosstone your whole life, right?"

"Near about!" she said, her cheeks squeezing into rosy balls.

"So you'd know most of the people in this town pretty well, then?"

"Oh, I should say so, love."

"Well," I affected casualness, "what do you know about Henry Kitteridge?"

"Henry?" she pursed her lips. She polished the countertop with a swirling motion. "Well – 'e's not your typical fellow. I guess when he were about seventeen, he run off to London to become an actor. He come back every so often to visit wif his old Dad, what used to run the White Stag, but," she winked at me, "I think that those visits were more for monetary than sentimental reasons, if y'get me drift. Him and his Dad never were close."

"Henry's father owned this pub?" I blinked rapidly, and looked around at the dark, musty room with new respect. This might have been my family business – if Henry and I were really related. "Then why doesn't Henry own it now?"

"Love, does 'Enry seem like the sort of man who could run a proper business? No, no – when his old Dad passed away, 'Enry sold the pub to me and Mr. Jenks. That were about twenty years ago, and we been runnin' it ever since."

I leaned my chin on my knuckles. "What did Henry do after that?"

She shrugged. "Well, you know 'Enry. He weren't never content to settle down in Mosstone as long as he had a quid. He went back to London and acted as long as he could. But then, a couple years back – well, I don't really know why, probably he were out of money – he come back, took the boards down off his old Dad's cottage, and set up this Mosstone Players bit. Oh, but I do love them pantomimes. Cor! I about laughed meself to death in that *Jack and the Beanstalk*. I can't wait to see his next one. I 'ope it's as funny as the last."

It would look somewhat suspicious to question her more in depth about Henry now that the conversation had reached its natural finish (after all – she might ask why it was I was so interested in Henry, and I didn't want to go there yet), so I picked up my fork and dug back into my lunch.

After a moment or two, though, Mrs. Jenks suddenly turned back to me with a concerned look on her face. "Oh, I meant to ask you - will you be wanting that room much longer?"

Something about the way she said it gave me an uneasy feeling.

I lay down my fork. "Why?"

"Well, I got a call from me son this morning. He's on leave from the Navy kind of unexpected-like, and when he comes home he sleeps in that room. I'm going to have to ask you to move out by tomorrow morning. Terrible sorry about the inconvenience."

"That's okay – I understand."

And that was when it hit me. The pub was the closest thing this town had to a hotel. As of tomorrow morning, I would have no place to stay.

* * *

I arrived at Henry's house, dragging my suitcases behind me, script under one arm. And the facts that I was no closer to my goal of finding out if Henry was my father, and that I would soon be homeless, *didn't help my anxiety level.*

I stopped at his doorstep, flipping through my script anxiously, hoping that he would focus on the other actors tonight so that I could work on solutions for some of my problems. I found my first big speech – the one that was giving me particular trouble – and read it under my breath: "If it were done when 'tis done, then 'twere well it were done…"

Someone walked past me and smacked my script out of my hands.

"Oops. Sorry," Daniel said, disappearing through the door.

As I bent to retrieve my script from the overgrown hedge, it occurred to me that I had yet another thing to stress about: the fact that it was becoming increasingly apparent Daniel hated me. Not just *mildly disapproved-of.* Not just *disliked. Hated.*

I guess I figured it out when he wrote "I hate you" on my script.

I couldn't even blame him for it. Because of me, Daniel had lost the best role he'd ever been cast in *and* his sparkly stage name – and I wasn't living up to either one.

But, regardless of whether I could understand it, it was becoming increasingly difficult to deal with. This "script knocking" business was just the latest – I'd also been tripped, stabbed with a dart and poked in the eye with a pool cue. If he were to launch an attack against any of my more sensitive areas – I might not be able to help an automatic, violent, rage reaction. And what then? Fight to the death? Over a role I didn't even *want*?

Holding my breath and counting to five, I jammed the script into my back pocket and stepped into the house.

Henry was standing in the living room on the couch – in a purple kimono, this time – and was talking to the others, who were seated on cushions in a semi-circle on the floor. When I stepped through the door, Henry spun around and snapped, "Ah, so the prodigal son has finally arrived, eh? Shut the door behind you before we all catch a cold."

I hung there in the doorway for a second, very close to just turning around and leaving. I gritted my teeth, shut the door, and then walked towards an un-claimed pillow. As I began awkwardly squatting to take my seat on it, Nora (or was it Dora?) looked up towards me and remarked, "You might as well not sit down. We're doing exercises."

I froze mid-squat. "Exercises?"

"All right, everyone," Henry said, clapping his hands. "On your feet! Scripts down, and double-up."

Nora took hands with Dora, Daniel stepped up to Mr. Smythe – and I was dreading the person I was about to be stuck with when Henry walked between us, shaking his head, saying, "No, no, no. I don't want you all with the obvious partner. Dora – Sophia. Nora – you can have Gladys, for variety. Trevor and I will be partners, and Durfrinson – why don't you partner with our boy Matthew?"

Daniel glared at me openly, his little eyes disappearing into slits. He walked over to my side stiffly and folded his arms, radiating hostility.

I wished, dearly, that we could have just run our lines tonight.

"All right," Henry said, once everyone had taken a place by their partner, "this is one of the techniques of Messrs. Sanford and Meisner. What I want you to do is stand face to face with your partner," he demonstrated by standing across from Trevor, "and repeat a word. You say it, and then they say it. You must repeat it exactly the way that they say it, without emotion, *without changing*, until something changes on its own."

What? I didn't get this – but everybody else seemed to, and Henry walked between them giving them their starting words. He gave Dora and Sophia "Scare", Gladys and Nora "High" – and then he walked up to Daniel and me, looked us both up and down and said, firmly, "Bone."

"But, Henry," I said as he turned away, "I don't understand…"

"*Bone*," Henry repeated, without a backward glance.

I faced Daniel awkwardly. His face was a mask of acne and disgust.

"Bone," he said, his voice monotone.

"Bone," I repeated, cautiously.

"Bone."

"Bone?" I said, raising my voice slightly.

"You're not supposed to change it until something changes on its own!" Daniel irritably snapped.

"But – how do I know when something has changed?"

"You just do," he said, then said again in perfect monotone, "Bone."

"Bone," I replied, keeping my voice empty this time. I felt like there was something very important about this exercise that I was simply missing – like, what the goal of it was, or what this magical spontaneous "change" would be, if neither of us changed anything purposefully.

We kept that up – I don't know, five, ten minutes? Nothing seemed to be changing. I was staring into Daniel's eyes and saying, "bone" and he was staring into mine and repeating it back.

No offense to Messrs. Sanford and Meisner, but I got absolutely nothing out of that exercise. As the minutes passed and I blankly repeated that word to Daniel, the only thing I was becoming aware of was this time would have been more productively spent practicing my lines. My mind began to wander. I stared at the red, irritated ring of acne around Daniel's lower lip, and then my eyes drifted over to the girls – Dora and Gladys were saying their word and giggling, while Sophia and Nora's exchange had morphed into a mirror exercise. Henry and Smythe were going at it with utter seriousness, repeating their word and gesticulating wildly with each utterance.

The word "bone" had begun to lose all meaning for me. I repeated it one last time, then decided that whether "something" had changed or not, I was going to make things change.

"Bone," Daniel said, still absolutely monotone.

"Bored," I said, rolling my eyes.

"Bone," Daniel repeated, not acknowledging my change.

"Birds," I said, shrugging.

"Bone."

"Biff," I said, pretending to punch myself in the chin, hoping I could break the tension. Instead, he just got a very set look on his face, seemed to struggle internally for a moment and said, "Biff."

Now we were getting somewhere. "Bite!"

"Bother," Daniel said, hotly.

"Bother," I repeated, going along with him.

"Bastard."

"Uh," I said, suddenly not liking where this was going.

"Bungler. Bore. Wait, we don't have to stick with B words," he said, with sudden vicious enthusiasm, "how about T? There are some great T words, like Thespian... Traitor... Torturer... Thief..."

"Okay, hang on a second..."

"Why, don't any of those words suit you?" Daniel said, sharply. "Funny, from my end they suit you just fine."

"Now, see here...!"

"Henry!" Daniel cried, raising his hand. "I want to change partners!"

"Change up," Henry said loudly. "Trevor – Gladys, Dora – Daniel, Nora and myself – Matthew and Sophia. Use the same words as before."

The Dragon Lady made a beeline for me, and my heart sank. I meekly raised my hand. "Uh, Henry? Can I be excused for a moment..."

"Matthew," Henry said, and pointed at the woman fiercely, "*Sophia*."

She looked me up and down and said, saucily, "Bone."

On her lips it was just wrong. Flushing uncomfortably, I repeated it. Then she suddenly reached out, put a hand on my shoulder and said, "Bride."

Wincing, I said, "Bride?"

"Bedfellows," she whispered, leaning towards me.

That was it.

"Excuse me," I muttered in a sickly fashion, and ran for Henry's bathroom. I switched on the light and bolted the door behind me, then sat down with my head in my hands.

It was almost nine o'clock. I hadn't eaten dinner, and I hadn't gotten a read-through of my lines which was what I needed most – and I wanted to go home.

Oh. Wait. I don't have a home. That's just great.

I got up, automatically washed my hands and stepped out of the bathroom, closing the door behind me. British bathrooms inexplicably seem to always have the light switch on the outside of the room, so I reached over to switch it off – only to grab the wrong one and switch on the hall light. Henry's hall was illuminated before me, and I noticed for the first time that he had *two* bedrooms.

Two bedrooms.

Say… What if Henry let me stay here?

It would give me some one-on-one time with Henry – something that up until this point I hadn't had. It would give me more chances to cautiously explore his belongings and look for clues. And perhaps he would help me run my lines.

It was ideal. It was more than ideal.

I felt as if a weight lifted off my shoulders, and switched off all the lights, running hastily back into the living room. In my absence, the exercise had dissolved into chatting. Henry was discussing something in depth with Sophia. I walked up and tapped gently on his shoulder, interrupting.

"What what what?" Henry said, turning around irritably.

"Henry, may I speak with you for a moment?"

"What is it lad? I haven't got all day."

I swallowed. "Look, Henry – I was wondering if I might ask you for some help…"

He shook his head briskly. "I'm sorry, lad – all of my money is spoken for with this production. I am *skint*, as they say."

"No, no," I said hastily, "I don't need money… It's just… Well,

I just lost my room at the pub, and I need a place to stay."

He looked at me blankly for a moment, and then it was as if a light bulb went off above his head. "*Oh!* I see! Well, don't worry, lad. I've got a room for you."

"Henry," I said, gratefully, "I can't thank you enough…"

"Don't even mention it," he said, clapping me on the arm, and turned back to Sophia. "Sophia, you've got a spare room, don't you? This young man needs a room – could you oblige him?"

She looked at me with those Dragon eyes. "I would oblige this young man any time of the day or night."

"It's settled, then! Matthew, you're staying with Sophia."

If it's possible for your soul to throw up, mine did.

* * *

The first thing I noticed was the smell, which hit me like a wall as I stepped through the door – a thick, overwhelming bouquet of patchouli and cigarettes. Do *all* theatre people smoke?

Sophia lived in a cottage not unlike Henry's – but smaller, more sparse. When I stepped in, that was what I noticed second: where every inch of Henry's is cluttered with evidence of a life lived, Sophia's is almost ascetically barren. The furniture – what there is of it – is gray and blends in with the walls and floor. There are no pictures, except for a large gray painting of a gray square with a foggy black line running horizontally through it. There was a tall, clear vase with a single white lily in it by the door, and that was about the extent of the decoration.

"I don't believe in worldly possessions," Sophia said, grandly, as she let me in through the door. "I only have what is necessary for me to get by."

I suppose I must have glanced at the picture or the flower at that point, because she added hastily, "The only non-essentials I own are things I find to be calming – and, hence, a necessity. I have always been a very taut, tension-filled being."

She shut the door behind me – bolting it and chaining it. I had a sinking feeling.

"Please," she said, looking me up and down, "make yourself at home."

She discarded her long, black coat, trailing it on the floor as she walked back towards the bedrooms. "Your room is back here – next to mine."

It was a small bedroom, barely big enough for the queen-sized bed that filled it. I squeezed into the room, wedging my suitcases into the narrow crack between the wall and the bed. The mattress was soft but there were no sheets or blankets.

"Thanks again for letting me stay here," I remarked, awkwardly standing pressed between wall and bed. "Do you mind if I borrow some sheets?"

"I wouldn't," she remarked, "but I haven't any. I don't believe in bed coverings; they are an unnecessary luxury imposed upon us by society. Our megalithic ancestors lived without sheets – and probably better for it, getting by on the strength of their *primitive instincts*." She eyed me significantly.

"Well, that's fine then!" I said hastily, diverting my attention to one of my suitcases – I flipped it open and pretended to be looking for something. "What time do you get up? I don't want to disturb your sleep."

"You can disturb my sleep any time, young man," Sophia murmured, leaning languidly against the doorframe. "But you needn't worry – I generally arise with the sun and do my Tai Chi."

"Fine," I said, not looking at her. "Just fine. Thanks again. I'll pay you rent for the room - whatever you think is fair." *Ach, a mistake.*

"Don't worry about it," she murmured. "I'll just consider this – a personal favor."

And with that, she slowly shut the bedroom door, giving me plenty of time to tell her to stay – which I did *not*, thank you very much.

As soon as the door was closed behind her, I crawled over the bed to the door and tried to lock it – but the lock didn't work. I picked up my suitcase and jammed it between the foot of the bed and the door, wedging it closed. I heaved a sigh of relief and threw myself back on the bed.

Okay – this arrangement wasn't going to work. Period. But – at least it would do for tonight, and keep me from having to sleep in a hedge somewhere. First thing tomorrow I'd go to Father Douglas and ask if anybody else in town – preferably some nice, wholesome family – was renting a room out.

I rolled over and dug into my other suitcase, pulling out my notebook and examining the list. I hadn't come any closer to my goals this evening – nor had I gotten to practice my lines or blocking at rehearsal – so I had to judge the entire evening a waste. I threw the notebook back into the case, reached over and switched off the overhead light, and lay back on the bed with my arm over my eyes.

A bead of sweat ran off of my arm into my eye. I suddenly became aware that I was sweating profusely, and it wasn't just stress – it was getting really, really hot in this room. Perhaps that was how Sophia made up for not having bed coverings; she cranked up the thermostat to volcanic temperatures.

I hadn't planned to undress at all (for safety reasons) – but the heat was getting unbearable. I took of my shirt, then undid my pants and kicked them off, and lay there panting in my underwear. I rolled around uncomfortably for the longest time, until finally it occurred to me that I might balance the temperature in the room by opening the window a crack. I sat up, pushed the window just a bit – then shoved it open the rest of the way and luxuriated in the cold breeze that wafted in across my hot, sweaty body. It made the room almost bearable. I lay down on my stomach and almost instantly fell asleep.

I don't know how long I slept before I heard a creak.

Oh God. The door opens outwards. I'm an idiot!!

I lay there with my eyes squeezed tight shut. Perhaps she was just checking on me. Perhaps she somehow realized the window was open and had come to shut it.

I heard the bedsprings creak and felt the bed shift as someone climbed on to it.

She's just climbing in to bed to crawl over and shut the window. That's all it is. That must be it.

I had almost convinced myself that she was really just in the room to close the window when I felt her silky nightdress press up against my back. Her lips hovered over my ear, and then she growled.

I'm glad the window was open, because before I knew what I was doing I was hurtling out of it into the darkness of the night. I landed on my bare feet like a cat and was halfway down the road before I realized that I was only wearing underwear. I realized that when – sprinting down the center of the road to goodness knows where – I found myself caught in the headlights of an oncoming car.

I froze for a moment like a deer, then dove off the road into the woods and hid behind a tree. I heard the car slow down and some concerned voices, but it kept going and in a moment I was alone.

So alone.

I stood there, shivering in the darkness, wondering what the hell I thought I was doing.

"Why," I said plaintively to myself, "couldn't I just have *told* Sophia that I wasn't interested in her advances and firmly asked her to leave the room? That would have been the adult thing to do."

I thought about it for a second and replied, *"But she's terrifying!"*

I couldn't help it! The fight-or-flight reflex had kicked in and I hadn't been able to control myself.

And now I was standing in the woods in my underwear, and it

was cold outside. Very cold. I could see my breath puffing out like clouds of smoke in the blue moonlight.

"Okay," I said out loud, hugging myself as I shivered. "The mature thing to do would be to walk right back there, calmly explain that I'm not interested, apologize if my actions in any way misled her – and get my stuff and leave."

I turned and started to march back towards Sophia's cottage, then spun around on my heel and marched back into the woods and leaned against my tree.

"Okay," I said, through chattering teeth. "I can't do it. That woman is crazy and I'm not going back there – not for my clothes, not for nothing!"

But I couldn't stand out in the woods all night. I already felt half frozen… I'd be dead of hypothermia before the morning.

My options were limited. I only knew where other three people in this town lived: Gladys, Mrs. Jenks, and Henry. As far as Gladys went, it exceeds the bounds of propriety for me to show up on Gladys's doorstep in my underwear (and anyway, the door would probably be answered by one of her parents). And as for Mrs. Jenks: while I felt that I could probably trust Mrs. Jenks to be discrete about my situation – my old bedroom was already spoken for. She had nowhere I could stay.

Which only left Henry.

It took me a long time to find my way back to Henry's cottage, as I was in an unfamiliar part of town in the dark – and, being in my underwear, had to keep hiding behind things whenever I thought a car might be coming or someone else approaching. When Henry's cottage was finally in sight, my heart leapt – his lights were still on. I skittered quickly across Henry's wet, cold lawn, banged my shin on his rusted bike and hopped onto his doorstep, shifting from foot to foot to keep my blood circulating. I knocked urgently, worrying about frostbite in areas where people simply shouldn't get frostbite. "Henry!"

I waited. Nothing.

"Henry – it's Matthew Ev… I mean, or Starr. Henry?"

I waited. Still nothing. He could be asleep.

I heard the dull roar of an approaching car, so I ran around the side of the house, ducking into the shadows. I waited there until the car had passed. I was about to return to Henry's front doorstep when I heard a peculiar, hollow, clacking sound in the darkness behind me.

For a moment I froze, terrified. But gradually fear became curiosity. I was in no position to be curious – but I was. Very, very slowly, I edged around the side of the cottage and peered into Henry's back yard.

Henry, still dressed in that purple kimono and house slippers, was smoking and playing croquet in the moonlight. By himself. As he lined up a shot with his croquet mallet, he was muttering something to himself, but I couldn't make out what he was saying.

There was something very… *peculiar*… about the scene being played out in front of me, and also very private. I felt like an intruder. I had a sudden sense that perhaps it would be best if I just went back to Sophia's… but I was just too cold for another naked run across town.

I had to do it. I gently cleared my throat.

Henry spun around, raising the croquet mallet into attack position. "Who's there?!"

"It's me," I said, meekly, hiding behind the edge of his cottage.

He squinted into the darkness, the cigarette dangling from his lips, and then slowly lowered the mallet. "Starr? What are you doing, hiding back there? Come out where I can see you."

I stepped out into the moonlight, shivering. To Henry's credit, the cigarette wobbled in his lips for a moment but he had no other visible reaction. At long last, he removed the cigarette, raised an eyebrow, and said, "Where are your trousers, man?"

"At Sophia's."

"Oh," he said, and then raised the eyebrow again.

"Henry," I said, through chattering teeth, "do you mind if we continue this conversation in the house?"

"Eh? Oh – I see what you mean. Oh, I suppose so. Come right in."

We went back around to the front of his house, and Henry allowed me to go into the bathroom and "freshen up" while he poured us both drinks. When I got back from running my hands and feet under the hot water tap, there was a pair of billowy sultan pants and a flowery white kimono waiting for me. Henry was in the kitchen, mixing whiskey sours with an expert hand.

"Henry," I began, but he shushed me with a wave of his hand.

"I don't want to know," he said, putting the glass in my hand. "Just tell me – can you go back to Sophia's tonight?"

I shook my head.

"Well then," he said, narrowly, "I suppose that means you need a different place to stay." *Finally.* What I wanted to hear.

He turned around and grabbed a phone off the wall. "Let me just dial Durfrinson."

I was unable to suppress a shudder. "Henry, I don't think that's a good idea…"

"Nonsense!" Henry said, then turning away and listening intently to the phone. He sat like that for a few long minutes and then hung up with a look of displeasure. "He didn't answer!"

Thank heaven for small miracles. I took a grateful gulp of my whiskey sour. It shocked my tastebuds for a moment but it felt very good on the way down.

"Gladys!" Henry cried, inspired. "Her parents have that big couch. It would be perfect for you!"

My mouth hung open slightly as he dialed.

"Gladys?" he said, "My dearest darling, I have a request. Know that big old couch of yours? Well, how about letting our boy Matthew stay on it?"

I couldn't hear what Gladys said in reply, but as he listened, Henry's expression went from delight to distraught.

"But why not?" he snapped.

He listened, and then abruptly wailed, "But I've got all my stuff in there!"

He listened for another moment or two, then said, "Very well," and hung open the phone.

Turning back to me, his face was a mask of bruised dignity.

"Well," he said, lifting his chin, "I have been failed by my right hand. Never is the day that I thought Gladys would fail to assist me in my hour of need."

"What did she say?" I asked, sipping my drink again.

"She said," he said, shaking his head as if it was the most ridiculous thing he'd ever heard, "that she thought you ought to stay here in my spare bedroom! I explained that I used that room for private purposes, but it was to no avail."

Good girl, Gladys! I felt a burst of warmth for her. I looked from my drink to Henry, then again, then finally asked, "Well? Is it all right if I stay here with you?"

Henry ran his hands through his silver hair, and then did some of the most exaggerated eye-rolling I've ever seen, as if this was the worst imposition he'd ever had to deal with. Finally he flung his hands in the air and said, "All right, all right! You can stay. But just for tonight! I don't like having my routines interrupted."

"Thank you!" I said, as he drank down the last of his whiskey sour.

"Oh, don't thank me," he said, bitterly, pouring himself a straight whiskey. "You can thank your number one fan, Gladys, at rehearsal tomorrow. It makes me sick. Just when you think you know a person…" He gulped down the glass and shuddered, then mutely gestured at me to follow him.

He led me back to that second room of his and laid his hand on the doorknob, taking a deep breath. "This is my work room, but you can have it for the night."

He threw the door open and we stepped in as he switched the light on.

I think I involuntarily gasped.

Surrounding the bed, on every available surface, were cat statues. Hundreds, and hundreds, and hundreds of them. They were all essentially the same – a little, bowling-pin like figure, bereft of arms and legs, with a cathead and huge staring eyes. The only difference was the size and color of the figures. Some were red, some were blue. Some were green with pink spots.

It wasn't until I noticed a sealed bucket of sculptor's clay an unpainted clay cat on a desk in the corner that I realized whom the artist was.

The room had a very unsettling quality. I felt like I was being stared at by two hundred eerie little eyes. It took me a moment or two to speak, and when I did, all I could manage was, "So."

"So what?" Henry said sharply, as if he was expecting mockery.

"So you like cats," I faltered.

He fished his cigarettes out of his pocket. "Yes, yes I do."
"But you don't own a cat."

He shook his head, and for the first time, a somewhat soft look came to his eyes. "No. I'd like nothing better to have a cat, but I'm terribly allergic. I also have a touch of asthma, and the allergies exacerbate the situation. My chest just closes up on me like a vice."

I can't imagine that the smoking helped very much either, but I didn't say so. It didn't seem right to pester him about it at the time. There was something just terribly sad about this little man in his empty house, desperately wanting a pet cat and never ever being able to get one. We stood in silence for a moment and I examined this new, more human side of Henry, until suddenly the iron bars in his eyes slammed back down and he raised an eyebrow at me.

"Well, there you have it," he snapped. "Don't touch any of them. And remember – you are here for ONE NIGHT ONLY!!"

He slammed the door behind him, and I was left alone. Alone, that is, except for the hundreds and hundreds of eerie, staring eyes.

CHAPTER SIX

Complications

At about ten in the morning, I was shaken roughly awake.

"Come on, then," Henry said irritably, releasing my shoulder when he saw that I was awake.

"What's going on?" I cried, extremely disoriented. I'd been in the middle of an intense dream and wasn't entirely sure where I was.

"We're going over to Sophia's to get your things."

"But..." I staggered out of bed, grabbing the wall for support. "But I don't have any clothes."

Henry sighed deeply, rolling his eyes again. "I just have to figure everything out, don't I? Very well – come in here."

I followed Henry meekly into his bedroom. If I thought the rest of the house was a mad jumble, his bedroom was about fifty times that level; there were paths to his bedside, to an old treadle sewing machine and to the closet. Every other inch of available floor space was covered in piles of *stuff* – newspapers, playbills, sheet music, books, costumes, props, masks – it was like the wide world of theatre had vomited fifty years of history into this room.

He switched on a dingy yellow bulb that hung from the ceiling, but it didn't do much for the place. Working his way down the narrow path to the closet, he managed to yank one of the doors partially open and peered in with his hand on his chin. He reached in and shifted some clothes around, then wedged himself through the narrow opening and disappeared.

After a few moments, I heard his muffled voice say, "What are your measurements?"

"Measurements? Uh," I rubbed my eyes foggily. "Thirty-two, thirty-two."

His face emerged. "Shoulders? Feet?"

"Shoulders - I have no idea. My feet are size ten in America – I don't know what that is over here..."

He disappeared again, and then a tight black turtleneck shirt was thrown into my face. As I was pulling it on, he emerged with something plaid draped over his arm.

"Well," he said, coughing on dust, "this is the only thing I have for your lower half."

He tossed me the plaid thing, which turned out to be a green and blue kilt. I eyed it for a moment, and then held it against myself. It ended just above the knee: a little high for my tastes.

"It can't be helped," Henry said sharply. "You're just too tall and wide for my trousers, and all the bigger costume trousers I have are in storage. You're just lucky that you're petitely-footed or I wouldn't have shoes for you either. Anyway – this will help you to get in character."

I felt like an absolute idiot when we stepped out of the house. I was never more thankful that Henry lived in a comparatively deserted area of town.

When we arrived at Sophia's cottage, I was hoping that we might find my bags outside on the lawn – but no such luck. Her little white door was bolted and the plain, white curtains drawn.

"Sophia," Henry sang, rapping on the door with his knuckles. "Sophia, dearest! *Caro mio!* May I come in?"

We waited. "Perhaps she isn't home," I remarked.

"Oh, she's at home all right." He rapped again. "Sophia, my dearest love! It is Henry. May I *entrée?*"

"Perhaps she just doesn't want to open the door," I said, darkly.

"Look," Henry snapped, "you go wait around the corner of the building there. She might open the door if it's just me."

I went around the side of the cottage, and Henry switched gears, pounding on the door with his fist. He kept this up for a good while, pounding and shouting at Sophia to let him in, until finally turned away, full of dignity, and strode to my side.

"Well, there you have it," he said, flicking an imaginary speck of dust off his shoulder.

"But – what do I do now?" I said, the full import of this situation finally dawning on me. "She has all my stuff!"

"Oh, I wouldn't be too concerned if I were you," Henry said, shrugging. "She's probably just – uh, well, you know – 'fury of a woman scorned' and all that. She'll get over it by tonight at rehearsal. Come on, let's go to the pub and get tea."

"But she has *all my stuff!*" I repeated. "My clothes, my wallet, my cellphone, my laptop, my –"

My notebooks with my notes on Henry. That was something I didn't want people to know about until I'd established that Henry really was (or wasn't) my father. Oh, God, what if she read them? What if she *told* somebody? What if she told *Henry? Oh God!!*

"Come now," Henry said brusquely. "Don't get your knickers in a twist. She has no interest in material possessions, as she doubtlessly told you. I'm sure after rehearsal tonight she'll have calmed down and she'll let us come and get your things."

Trying to cover my discomfiture, I said hastily, "But how am I supposed to find another place to stay without my wallet?"

Henry rolled his eyes. He seemed to do that a lot when I was around.

"Oh well," he said dramatically, "I *suppose* you can stay for one more night!"

During our lunch at the pub, Henry read the paper and talked sports with Mr. Jenks. I tried to follow the conversation, but I know nothing about British teams (all this talk of "Chelsea" and "Manchester United" was so much gibberish), so I kept quiet and put away my Shepherd's Pie while I secretly worried about Sophia.

What would I do if she revealed the contents of my notes to Henry? Well, if Henry wasn't my father, it would make me look stupid and possibly like a bit of a stalker, but I didn't see it being a big deal. Matthew had a dumb theory, Matthew was wrong, nobody's any worse off. They'd probably all have a good laugh at my expense, and that was the finish of it.

But what if he *was* my father? How would he react? I suppose that depended on whether Henry knew he had fathered a child or not. If he didn't know he had fathered a child, but remembered mother and his relationship with her, it might be a terrible shock. Not to mention cause him horrible, remorseful feelings about having missed my childhood and never been there for me...

On the other hand, if he *knew* he had fathered a child with my mother in America – why the hell hadn't he recognized me?

Then it struck me. What if he *did* recognize me? What if he was pretending not to know me because he didn't *want* to be my father? The very thought of it chilled my heart. Perhaps he'd known all along – he just didn't want any part of me.

I realized suddenly that I had been sitting there, frozen with laden fork of mushy peas poised halfway to my mouth, for some time. This wouldn't have been so bad if it wasn't for the fact that

Henry had noticed and was staring back at me over his newspaper with a raised eyebrow.

"May I ask what your problem is?" he said, steadily.

"Nothing," I said hastily, my voice quavering. I put down my fork and looked away. "Nothing at all."

"Then stop staring at me like that," he said, raising the newspaper up between us. "Freak."

I should ask him now. I should push away my plate, look over at him, and ask him if he was my father. That would save all the trouble of waiting to see if Sophia revealed my secrets or not – and I would finally be achieving the whole purpose of my coming to this place.

It was the right moment.

"Henry," I said, a bit too loudly.

He looked up. "Yes?"

My voice caught in my throat. I cleared it. "Henry... I notice that you toured America doing *Hamlet*."

"Uh huh." He turned the page of his paper without looking up.

"You were in Chicago."

"That's right. I was there for three months and had my wallet stolen three times. Beastly city."

"Well..." I cleared my throat again. "Did you ever know a woman named Anna Jay Johnson?"

At this, Henry froze. His gaze retreated inward momentarily, and then he slowly folded the paper and put it aside.

"Anna Jay Johnson," he repeated, rubbing his chin. "Anna Jay. Anna Jay. It doesn't ring any bells. What did she look like?"

I described her quickly as she would have looked then. Short, dark-skinned, freckled, with a fat braid of hair. At the mention of the freckles, Henry's eyes suddenly lit up.

"Of course!" he said, snapping his fingers. "There was a girl who looked like that who worked for the company that was sponsoring our show. I remember her distinctly because of the darkish skin and the freckles – thinking what an odd combination it was. Didn't she have green eyes?"

I swallowed dryly. "Yes."

"Striking girl," Henry said, nodding at his memory. "Quite striking. Of course, I didn't know her as Anna Jay Johnson; she was going by 'Ladybird' as a lark, and I never knew her actual name." He looked at me suspiciously, and I wondered if he was suddenly noticing my darkish skin, my freckles and my greenish eyes. "Why do you ask?"

I don't know how I ever got the words out.

"She was my mother."

Henry sucked on a tooth for a moment, looking me up and down. "Well. Small world, isn't it!"

Then he picked up his paper and flipped to the crossword.

This wasn't the reaction I had hoped for. It wasn't an answer. Was that an, *I don't know I'm your father,* or an *I don't want to be your father?*

"Did you know her -- well?" I persevered.

"Hm?" Henry said, distractedly marking the crossword. "What's an eight letter word for crustacean?"

"*I said,* did you know her well?" My voice went up a pitch.

"Oh, not really," he said, not looking up. "As I said, she worked for the company that was sponsoring us. We might have had a couple brief chats, maybe shared had a drink or something. But no."

"You seem to remember her pretty well for someone you... didn't know," I said, feeling agitated. I jabbed violently at my leftovers.

"What difference does it make?" He lowered the paper suddenly and looked at me with a piercing gaze. "Do you have your lines memorized?"

The question caught me off-guard. "Uh… Well…"

"Well *what?*" That eyebrow of his arched suspiciously. "Do you or don't you?"

"Well – no."

"No?!" he gasped. "You *don't?* The play is in less than two weeks and you don't have your lines memorized yet?"

"It's like memorizing a book word for word!" I cried. "A book in a foreign language, at that!"

"Now, see here," Henry said, folding his newspaper and putting it aside, "you need to get that play memorized by tonight. *Tonight*, you understand?"

"But I don't even have my script…"

"Jenks, put this on my tab. Starr, we are going back to my house *right now* to run your lines. You will have your part memorized by tonight if it kills you."

CHAPTER SEVEN

The Scottish Play

Sitting on Henry's toilet that evening, I realized I still had all three possibilities before me: first, that he *wasn't* my father; second, that he *was* my father, but didn't know; and third, that he was my father, but didn't *want to be*.

"Starr!" Henry shouted, pounding on the bathroom door. He flicked the bathroom light on and off from its weird, outside-the-bathroom position. "Are you quite finished? It's time to get memorizing!"

I slowly pressed the heels of my hands into my eyeballs – and then, I realized the fourth possibility. It had been there all along but I dared not name it until now: the possibility that Henry really was my father – and that *I didn't want him to be*.

I flushed and washed my hands.

We spent – I don't even know how many – hours, Henry yelling my cues and me trying to say my lines. With the exception of a couple of my big speeches, I had the play mostly down by the time rehearsal rolled around, although Henry had lost his voice from yelling at me.

"That's enough," he said, his voice a dry, raspy squeak, as he collapsed into his armchair. "Someone's at the door. Answer it like a good lad while I have a fag."

"A what?"

"A *fag*," he said, holding out a cigarette. "Now *answer the door.*"

It was Gladys, of course, in an oversized Union Jack sweatshirt.

"Oh, hi, Gladys!" I exclaimed. It was a relief to see her. It seemed like she was the only person I'd met on this excursion who wasn't trying to hurt my brain in some way. But she didn't answer – she just gave me this look that I could not fathom and silently drifted into the kitchen to make a pot of tea. I was going to follow and talk to her for a few minutes (it seemed like I hadn't actually spoken to her very much lately), but Henry stopped me with a hand in the center of my chest and said, "Say the 'tomorrow and tomorrow' speech."

I failed of course, and he was hoarsely yelling at me again when Smythe and Daniel arrived.

"Mr. Branagh got his lines memorized yet?" Daniel said, his lip curling at me as he walked past.

"Never mind him," Henry said, coldly. "Have you got *yours* down?"

Daniel shuffled uneasily. "Well – pretty close…"

"I thought as much. After the girls get here I'm going to…" He didn't even finish the threat – just gave him a look that sent him scurrying, and then subsided into a coughing lump on the couch.

Nora and Dora arrived in matching pink jumpers, and then we were waiting on Sophia.

We weren't terribly surprised when fifteen-after rolled around, because (as Henry remarked) it was more surprising for Sophia to be on time than for her to be late. But Henry began to get impatient when she was a half hour late. And by the time she was a full hour late, he was pacing the room frantically.

"All right," he said at last, stabbing out his cigarette, "we can't wait any longer. Gladys, you read Sophia's parts until she shows up."

With an anxious glance, Gladys scooped up her tech script and walked up to my side. She had suddenly gone a rather pallid shade of white. Noticing that (which seemed unusually sensitive for him) he suddenly said, "No, dear, no. That's okay. You have a seat. Um…" He looked around the room, tapping his chin. "Everybody but the star should have a seat."

I found myself standing in the center of the room alone, surrounded by hostile stares.

Henry walked up to me, still tapping his chin. He looked me up and down, circled me thoughtfully once or twice, and then said abruptly, "Start saying your lines. When you get stuck – just say a rough approximation of what you think your lines are, and go on."

I swallowed hard and said, "So foul and fair a day I have not seen."

He snapped his fingers. "Blah blah blah, three witches, etc. Next line."

"Speak if you can: what are you?" And then my mind went blank. I struggled – I thought hard – I mentally dragged my fingernails through the crevices of my brain, looking for the tiniest scrap of dialogue – and came up empty.

Suddenly a hideous, muffled, raspy feminine voice by my elbow said, "All hail, MacBeth, hail to thee, thane of Glamis, thane of Cawdor, thou shalt be king hereafter!"

There was a burst of unexpected laughter from my cast members -- I looked down at my elbow and was startled to see Henry holding up a tiny, terrifying old woman puppet – it looked like it had been carved out of a potato. I was so taken aback that I automatically spat out my next line, *"Stay, you imperfect speakers, tell me more…"*

And we went on that way. I just kept on going, saying as much of my lines as I could remember – while Henry acted out every other character, with puppets, masks, cat statues – an old sandwich – a broom – plants – anything and everything that he had around the house. And, my god, it was *hilarious*. I have never seen anything as funny as that – or a performance like that! It was amazing – *he* was amazing! And he wasn't even looking at a script! The rest of the cast was rolling with laughter – literally – until finally I was killed at the end of the play and Henry stood, victorious, fern in hand, over my body.

The rest of the crew burst into spontaneous applause. Granted, we're only talking about five people – but it was completely genuine. I looked up at Henry (who was standing over me with a boot in the middle of my chest) – and saw sweat on his face, and his chest heaving as he attempted to suck in enough air to make up for what he'd been spitting out for the past hour – but also saw something else, something I had not seen on him up until this point.

He was smiling. There was a light in his eyes that I hadn't seen before. An honest, *happy* light – pleased, delighted – and maybe just even a little *modest* – but it was a secret happiness.

And then like a light, it switched off.

"All right, my loves," he said, stepping off me, and offering me a hand to pull me up. For such a dainty fellow, he was easily able to heave me to my feet. "That's all the fun and games we're allowed for one evening. Everyone retrieve your scripts, and we'll start from page one. No, wait, scrap that – take five – I've got to get some air."

And then he flew out his front door, cigarette already hanging from his lips.

"Matthew!" Gladys exclaimed, walking over and punching me in the shoulder as I shuffled to the corner where my script lay. "You got through the script without stopping! Good job!"

"I think I might not have said everything I was supposed to…"

"I doesn't matter. You kept going. That's what counts!"

"I did, didn't I?" I felt a little bit impressed with myself, but then looked out the window at Henry – who was pacing the yard at a frenetic speed and already lighting his second cigarette. "But it was really him, wasn't it? I mean – I've never seen anything like that."

"Now you know why I hang around with Henry," she said following my gaze. "He really is something special."

"Why isn't he on TV or in movies or something?"

"I think he's done that kind of thing – but I think he just likes the stage. He said there's nothing like having an audience right there, feeling their response and the energy that rolls off them when you do something that pleases them..."

I looked out the window at Henry, and suddenly it struck me what a profoundly lonely lifestyle that was. To only live and get satisfaction out of life by desperately sucking every last drop of joy out of the approval of strangers? Thank god I never had the acting bug. It was a devastating illness.

And then I looked back at Gladys and cocked my head. "And why do you do theater, Gladys? As a crewmember you don't even get the 'energy' of the audience. What's in it for you?"

She gave me a mysterious look and said, in an odd, singsong voice, "Oh, I guess I just like hanging around with actors," and drifted away into the kitchen.

The phone on the wall jangled – and abruptly Henry burst back in through the front door, heedlessly throwing his cigarette stub into Daniel's drink. "That's probably Sophia on the phone – I have to take this. Talk amongst yourselves, children."

He snatched the phone off the hook and disappeared into the darkness of his hallway. There was a hushed conversation (that all of us strained to hear).

"No," I heard him say. "No. My dearest... *Caro*... That's foolishness. Sheer foolishness. You can't mean... You can't..."

There was silence for a few moments, and then abruptly Henry squared his shoulders and walked back into the room, dangling the phone from his hand carelessly. He looked from face to face, and then hung the phone on the wall without a word.

"What was it?" Gladys asked.

"Was it Sophia?" Daniel asked, seeming genuinely concerned. "What did she say?"

Henry kept his lips pressed together for a long moment, then shrugged his shoulders carelessly and walked towards the door. "Oh, nothing, nothing – it was just a bit of foolishness."

Very carefully affecting casualness, he slipped into his coat and hat. "Uh, I'm going to step out for a few moments."

"Where are you going?" Dora and Nora said in unison, their brown eyes huge in their pale faces.

"I'm just going down the road to go have a little talk with Sophia."

Smythe sipped from a teacup, returned it to the saucer in his other hand and remarked, "She's quit the show, hasn't she."

"Nonsense!" Henry said sharply, his cloak flying behind him. "She just has personal issues going on at the moment, and I'm going to go and address them for her. Now, while I'm gone I want you to all to run lines, understand? Gladys, make sure they run their lines while I'm gone. You stand in for Sophia where necessary."

And with a theatrical swish of his cloak, he was gone out the door, leaving the other occupants of the room in an unhappy mix of confusion and foreboding.

"I don't like this," Daniel remarked, biting his thumbnail. "I don't like this one bit."

"She wouldn't quit," Dora remarked. "That doesn't make one bit of sense."

"Why would she do it?" Nora said, putting her head on her twin's shoulder.

I was disinclined to offer a theory. I knew exactly why Sophia would quit. They couldn't blame me for that, though, surely… Surely! Of course, that wasn't my only concern. What if Sophia showed Henry the contents of my notebook? What would he think? What would he say?

I was very relieved when Gladys stood up with a businesslike air and lifted her technical script.

"Well, whatever the situation, we need to run lines as Henry asked us to. Shall we start from scene one?"

I stood up hastily. "Let's."

"But why would she quit?" Dora pursued, unwilling to drop the topic. "She's Lady M. That's like the best role in the show. I don't understand."

Smythe was sitting over in the corner. He swished the tea around in his teacup in a leisurely fashion and took a delicate sip. "I might know why."

I felt a cold chill down my spine.

"Why should you know more than anyone else?" Daniel asked him with a vaguely hostile air, jamming his script into his belt.

Smythe looked up blandly. "You forget, children… As a mature woman, Ms. Sophia is more likely to seek out someone her own age to confide in. She called me this afternoon and explained the situation to me."

"Why, then?" Dora and Nora cried in unison.

"Lines," Gladys said, vainly rapping on her script with her knuckles. She looked at me with an expression like a drowning man. She had lost control of them and she knew it. "Everybody, we need to work on lines…"

Henry chose that moment to push the door open and step back in with a rather subdued expression on his face.

I searched his face urgently for some sign that Sophia had shown him my notebooks – but there was none. He didn't even look at me.

We waited for a moment in silence while Henry lit up a cigarette. Then, with a broad wave of his hand, he announced, "Well, I cut Sophia from the show."

There was a moment of palpable confusion from all regions.

"But -!" Daniel cried.

"But Mr. Smythe said Sophia quit," Dora said, and then looked at him with narrowed eyes. "He said she called him and said so."

"Then Mr. Smythe has been fibbing," Henry said, his eyebrows arching irately. "I cut Sophia from the show."

"Why would you do that?" Nora cried. Mr. Smythe was already growing beet-red in the face and obviously about to loudly disagree with his word being questioned...

"Now, see here," Henry said, climbing up on the arm of his couch and looking down on us, "I am the director. I make the artistic choices for this show. If you offer me any back-chat, I will cut you. That is what happened to Sophia and I would thank all of you to learn by her example."

"But what are we going to do?" Daniel moaned, covering his eyes. "We can't go on without Sophia."

"We'll make do," Henry said.

"But we haven't got a Lady Macbeth," I remarked.

For a moment, nobody realized what had happened – until we saw Henry's face a ghastly gray and I threw my hands over my mouth.

"Hatfield," Henry said hoarsely. "You said the name of the Scottish play. How *could* you."

"Surely it doesn't count," Gladys said hastily. "I mean, he only said Lady Mac –"

"Not you too!" Henry shrieked. "Out! Out! All of you!! *Get out of my house!!*"

"But, rehearsal," I said, weakly.

"Forget rehearsal! I'm canceling this production!! Get OUT!!"

We trooped out of Henry's house and stood on his lawn – he slammed the door shut behind us.

"Well, that's it, then," Daniel said.

"Good job, young man," Mr. Smythe said, slapping me between the shoulders. "You took us from a well-mounted production all the way to utter destruction in less than two weeks. Congratulations."

Dora and Nora each kicked one of my ankles and left me hopping in pain, and then – because there was nothing else to say – my cast members began to disperse. In just a few moments, only Gladys and I were left. She was mutely replacing her notebooks and script in her bag.

Well, that was that, then. Henry had thrown me out. There would be no show, he would be ruined – and, I would never truly find out if he was my father or not. Plus, I no longer had a place to stay, and I'd lost all of my things – including my wallet, cellphone and passport. How would I even get home?

I stood there, miserably, for a few long moments, icy breeze wafting up my kilt, before I was finally able to say, "I'm sorry, Gladys."

"Sorry?" she said, looking up with a genuinely confused expression on her face. "What for?"

"For everything," I said, my eyes sinking to my feet. "For coming here and ruining this show."

"Oh, come now," she said, gently punching my arm. "This show isn't ruined."

"The leading lady is gone, and the show is cancelled because I said – that word," I said, gazing at my feet. "How is it not ruined?"

Her sweet little face smiled up at me. "Walk with me, Matthew."

We walked out of Henry's yard and down the quiet country lane. I had no idea how quiet the night could be. Coming from the city, there's always some kind of noise – but out here, with cold fall weather quieting all the frogs and insects for the winter, it was as absolutely silent. The only sound was the rocks on the dirt road crunching beneath our feet as we walked.

After a few moments, Gladys finally spoke again, stopping in the road and looking up at me. In the pale moonlight that stripped the scene of color, and with those big eyes of hers and that round, simple face, she looked like a silent movie heroine: childlike, sincere and adorable.

"Don't take Henry so seriously, Matthew," she said, in her gentle voice. "He only 'cancelled' this production because he's superstitious. I can guarantee you that he'll phone everybody up tonight and have the show put back together by tomorrow – but he'll consider it a different production so that the 'curse' can't strike it. You see?"

Those big eyes looked up at me imploringly, glittering in the moonlight – and I had a sudden, intense desire to kiss her. I don't know where it came from. I suppressed it quickly, biting my lip and looking away.

"I see." I swallowed, looking up at the night sky. "I guess that does make a kind of sense – but I wish he'd actually said that if that was what he meant."

"If he *said* it the curse would know and it wouldn't count! You don't understand Henry, Matthew."

"I certainly don't."

"Don't worry. I can almost promise that you'll hear from him before the night is out. Go back to your room and get some sleep."

That cold breeze went up my kilt again, fluttering it around my knees. A-la Marilyn Monroe I modestly held it down in the important areas and shook my head at Gladys. "I can't do that."

"Why not?"

"I was staying with Henry. Even if things do work out tomorrow, I doubt he's going to let me back in tonight."

"Oh." Gladys slipped her hand into mine. "Well, you'd better come with me, then."

A warning bell went off. "Gladys…"

"You can sleep on the sofa," she said, leading me down the road with childlike simplicity. "Mum and Dad won't mind one bit."

"Are you sure?" I said, uncertainly.

"I'm positive! Oh, come now, Matthew. What other options do you have?"

"Well…" I contemplated it for a moment. I really *didn't* have any other options.

"Exactly," she said, reading my mind. "Now, come on. I bet you haven't even had supper. We'll rustle up some tucker and then you can get a good night's sleep."

Like a small child, Gladys led me by the hand back to their small house. Her parents were already asleep when we got there, so she led me to the kitchen and quietly made us ham sandwiches and cocoa. She talked to me for a long time about random things – about her father's job at a local dairy, a pet parrot she'd once had, her hopes for another season of a TV show she liked that I'd never heard of. Feeling like I ought to share something about myself, I told her about my job at the Dynex Corporation, about my fondness for Silent-Era movies. To my surprise, she was able to converse about this quite knowledgeably – something fairly unusual in people her age (and, if I'm honest, mine). After she recognized the name of the admittedly obscure Harry Langdon, I burst out, "How old are you, Gladys?"

"What, me?" She shrugged. "Thirty-one."

"Holy crap!" I said, then added hastily, "I mean, there's nothing wrong with that – nothing at all. It's just… You're my age. I thought you were like eighteen."

Gladys changed the subject; I had probably made her uncomfortable by talking about her age. She brought up Charlie Chaplin, and eventually – through discussion of his film *The Kid*, my favorite movie – I found myself talking about my Mom, and my step-Dad, Harry Evans. I told Gladys how Mom had raised me, how she had always taken responsibility for her own mistakes and raised me to do the same, how she'd been such an integral part of my life, and then had quietly, like a party guest who doesn't want to bother the host, slipped out of it.

"She sounds like she was an amazing woman," Gladys said, staring into her cup. "Is Harry gone, too?"

"He went while I was in college," I said quietly. I felt a catch in my throat. Until that moment, I hadn't realized quite how much I missed them both. It left an awful, hollow feeling in my chest.

That couldn't be allowed. I dealt with it the way I had been dealing with it since their funerals – by quickly changing the subject to a less emotionally-charged one; in this case, food. We discussed the respective merits of different universal fast-food chains until almost midnight.

"It's late." She put our dishes in the sink, and then led me to their small living room, sat me on the couch and brought me a thick, soft, yellow blanket. I put up my feet and kicked off my shoes – and before I could protest, Gladys was tucking me in.

"There you are," she said, quietly, enfolding me in a soft, yellow cocoon of warmth. She hesitated for a moment, then said, "Well, I'd best be off to bed me-self, or I'll never be up in time for work. Goodnight, Matthew."

She walked to the doorway and switched the light off.

"Gladys?"

She turned around hastily, switching the light back on. "Yes,

Matthew?"

"Uh…" I wasn't sure I wanted to ask the question that had formed in my mind – but it had been a strange enough evening, and we had shared enough, that I felt emboldened to do it. "Gladys – are you and Henry… dating?"

"Me and *Henry?*" she said, as if it was the most absurd thing she'd ever heard of. "No, Matthew. I…"

She hesitated for a long moment, leaning against the doorframe and staring at the floor, before finishing. "I did *like* Henry. When I first joined the troupe, I mean. He was so – not like any man I'd ever met before. But, I guess he noticed how I felt, because in that fine, gentlemanly way of his, he took me aside and explained that he was very flattered, but that he made it a rule not to strike up that kind of relationship with someone who was involved in a production with him. So I gave him up." There was silence for a long moment. "Why do you ask?"

"No reason," I said, hastily. "Just curious."

"I see." She switched off the light. "Goodnight, Matthew."

"Goodnight, Gladys."

The darkness enfolded me, and I heard Gladys's feet pad down the short hallway to her room – and I heard the door close behind her. Then I heard a lock turn.

Whew. Well, at least I could sleep comfortably tonight knowing that no one was going to try to molest me while I was unconscious. I pulled the blanket up to my chin and, for the first time since I'd been in England, I totally relaxed. Talking with Gladys had been nice – it reminded me of talking with Patty, except that Gladys was far less vitriolic. Contemplating this pleasant fact, I was asleep in seconds.

Sometime later I was awakened by the sound of a cell phone going off in a different room. I heard Gladys's muffled voice answer it and say "Henry" – and I knew that she had been right, that Henry had called to reinstate the show, and that everything was going to be all right.

It wasn't until I woke up in the morning that things began to sink in.

I woke up with my face pressed into the musty brown cushions of the couch. They had the musty smell of old potato chips, dog and socks. I opened my eyes and stared at them in an unfocused way.

Perhaps it would have been better if the show hadn't been reinstated.

For one thing – I didn't actually *want* to do it. I'm not an actor; I have no business starring in a production of a Shakespeare play. This was a disaster in the making. And who knows if Sophia was returning to the show or not? Whether she did or not there were serious drawbacks…

I was reminded suddenly of Gladys's admission of her feelings for (and rejection by) Henry, and that led my thoughts suddenly in a different direction. Henry claimed (at least for the purposes of rejecting Gladys) that he had a rule about not getting involved with people who worked on his shows. Henry told me that my mother had been semi-involved with that production of *Hamlet* -- did that mean that he couldn't have been involved with my mother?

There was no way of knowing. He might have instated that rule after Mother – or not instated it at all, simply making it up as an excuse to kindly turn-down Gladys. But if it were true, then something was certain: this entire trip, all the money I'd spent and all the suffering I was going to do for this show, were a total and utter waste.

With this depressing thought in mind I rolled over – and discovered a stout older man seated in an armchair and staring at me intently.

The oily gleam of shower-less early morning shone on his balding, somewhat combed-over, head; he was dressed in a pair of rumpled pajamas; he held a steaming mug in his hand.

"Ah," I said, affecting casualness, sitting up on the couch and trying to smooth my wild hair down. "You must be Gladys's father.

I'm Matthew Evans."

He said nothing, which was somewhat disconcerting. He took a long sip of his coffee or tea or whatever it was, and then went back to staring at me expressionlessly.

"Gladys might not have mentioned me," I said, hastily, wishing suddenly that I wasn't wearing a kilt. "I'm an American and I'm involved with Henry Kitteridge's production of – the Scottish play. I needed a place to stay last night and Gladys offered me your couch. I hope that's all right."

Gladys's father absorbed this for a long moment. He took another long swig of his beverage, and then said in a low, gravelly voice, "Now, see 'ere, young man. Have you got any *designs* on my daughter?"

"No!" I cried, then added in a more level voice, "I mean, no. No. We're just friends."

"Good." Gladys's father absorbed this for another few moments, and then he heaved himself out of the chair and waved me towards the kitchen. "Have a cuppa."

I went into the kitchen with him, where Gladys's mother was pouring me a bowl of cereal. She greeted me pleasantly, made me a cup of tea, and began asking me about America and where I came from and what the flight was like. She was very much an older, plumper version of Gladys. It seemed like forever before Gladys finally emerged from her bedroom. Her eyes were a bit puffy and red – allergies, I thought.

"Well, there you are, young lady," Gladys's mother said, getting up and reaching for a second bowl. "It's about time you got up. You're almost late for work and you've kept your young man waiting forever."

"Well, either way you'd better get a move on," her mother said. "Let me pour you some tea."

"I don't want anything," Gladys said. "Matthew, let's go."

Hastily gathering myself, I thanked her parents for their generosity and ran after Gladys out the front door.

"Gladys," I said, following her at a trot, "did I offend you somehow?"

"Why should I be offended?" Gladys snapped. "You've said nothing that should offend me. I have no good reason to be upset."

I'd heard that one before. "But you do seem to be upset."

She stopped mid-stride and turned her face away from me for a long moment. After a bit, she took a long, shaky breath and turned back to me with a smile on her face.

"I'm sorry, Matthew," she said, "I'm just in a bad mood this morning, I suppose. Don't mind me."

"Well, okay," I said. "By the way – where are we going?"

"Oh, I'm sorry – I forgot to tell you. Henry called last night and the show's on again: he wanted us to meet him at the pub this morning for some notes before I head on to work."

"Well, that's another relief."

Or was it?

* * *

"How are we supposed to do this play without Sophia?"

Henry, a cigarette dangling from his lips, was unperturbed by Daniel's question. "Simple. We will simply – simplify."

"Simplify?" Mr. Smythe said, nonplussed. "We've already cut out half of the dialogue in this show. What else can we cut?"

Henry just narrowed his eyes and remarked, "Pencils, please."

We got out our pencils and Henry liberally cut and re-assigned lines until Lady M. was no longer in our production of the Scottish play. The part where the Lady convinces my character to kill the king was now a rather bizarre soliloquy on my part.

"You see?" Henry said, pleasantly crushing his cigarette underfoot. "Good as new."

CHAPTER EIGHT

The Unexpected

One week to the show. Gladys made posters; I ran a hundred and fifty copies of them on the library photocopier and then slapped them on every post in town. Gladys and her "Mum" sewed costumes; I modeled. In evenings we rehearsed frantically, trying to learn the new lines and scenes generated by our ever-lessening cast. I was so busy that I forgot how stressed out I was.

Almost.

My time in England was drawing to a close. I was no nearer to figuring out if Henry was my father than I had been on the day I showed up in town. I still hadn't gotten my wallet, passport or other belongings back from Sophia. I had been wearing the same clothes for a week – that black turtleneck and ridiculous kilt. Whenever I walked into a building I heard hushed conversations questioning whether I was eccentric or just slow.

Those things were bugging me a little, you might say. That, and the fact that the day was drawing nearer and nearer to the performance of this horrible show. I was a corpse when I said my lines – I knew it. But there was nothing I could do about it. My carefully rehearsed movements were stiff and awkward. Henry fed me my lines (that's where he says it with the emotion and tempo it's supposed to have and I just try to copy him) and it wasn't working. But, cripes! I had a perfectly good excuse…!

"No no NO!" Henry shouted, slamming his script down on the counter. He got up, walked over to the corner of the pub where we were rehearsing, put his arm over my shoulder and slowly led me aside. "Matthew, as you're an actor in this show, you might want to try something other actors do – it's called acting. It might help with your performance."

"Henry," I said sharply, balling my hands into fists at my side, "I am *not an*…"

"Yes yes yes," he said, waving my protest away. He'd heard it enough lately. "Look. Generally I am not in favor of this technique, but it might help. I want you to have a sense-memory."

"A what?"

"Look. When you get to the bit about life being just a walking shadow and so on, you've just been told that your WIFE is DEAD. You need to have some emotion. So, when you get to the line, 'She should have died hereafter' I want you to think of a situation in your past where you were sad, or angry, or worried. Any of those emotions would fit. All right? All right. Places, everyone!"

I went back to my place at the barstool that was acting as my battlement. Daniel came up to me and gave me my cue, "The Queen, my Lord, is dead!"

It was hard to be sad about the Queen being dead, especially since she no longer appeared in this show – but I tried to think of something sad anyway. Mother dying? No, no, I couldn't handle that right now. What about Harry dying? No, I couldn't handle that either. What about nervous? I was nervous about my job, nervous about this show, nervous about whether Henry was my father or not… God, I could do nervous. I could definitely do nervous.

After a few moments, Henry interrupted my nervous thoughts

by announcing, "Matthew. Your lines will be much more effective if you actually *speak*."

I snapped my mouth shut and then squawked in a wholly unnatural voice, "She *should* have died *hereafter!*"

Henry clapped his hand over his face. He lifted it a few moments later - just in time to see a cold blast of air from the door lift my kilt.

The girls all screamed and hid their faces.

The doors of the pub had burst open and a diminutive figure in a long black coat had entered. While my hands darted down to hold the kilt in place, Henry leapt from his seat and cried, "Lord Hatfield! What an unexpected pleasure!"

The small figure drew a striped muffler down from his face, exhibiting that withered, cheery, mustached smile. "I do hope I'm not disturbing the show."

"Not at all, not at all, sir!" Henry cried, ushering him towards the bar. "Jenks! A bottle of wine for Lord Hatfield!"

"No, no," Lord Hatfield said pleasantly, rubbing his hands together, "that won't be necessary. I just thought I'd dash in this evening and see how it all was going."

I thought I saw Henry blanch slightly under the cheerful mask he was wearing, but before anyone else could perceive it he was shaking his head.

"Oh, Lord Hatfield. As much as I would be delighted to show you our progress..." Behind Lord Hatfield's back, Henry waved us further into the corner, "...I rather feel that showing it to you at this point would *ruin the surprise*. After all, there's only one more week before the performance."

The scene of the play (what there was of it) quickly disintegrated. Henry asked Smythe, who was evidently a friend of Lord Hatfield's, to come up and speak to him, so Daniel, Gladys, the —oras and I were left in the corner to contemplate our fears.

"This can't be good," Daniel muttered.

"Shush," Gladys said. "Look – they're all smiling. It's going to be fine."

"If he insists on seeing us perform," Daniel whispered at her, and then cast a significant glance at me, "we are finished. He'll pull the funding."

"Shush," Gladys snapped. "Play your darts."

Daniel picked up the red darts and began sending them, highly inaccurately, into the dartboard. I picked up the black darts and forgot myself in the game – concentrated on that sharp point sticking in the red circle in the center of the board. I swear that there is nothing more satisfying than the sound of a dart hitting home. I was so intent upon the game (which I was absolutely pulverizing Daniel at, by the way) that I didn't realize a small, round shape had appeared at my elbow.

As the last of my darts smacked home, Lord Hatfield began to applaud. "Jolly good show! Jolly good! You're quite the darts player, young man."

"Thank you, sir," I said modestly, retrieving my darts from the board.

"When you're up at the manor, Mr. Hatfield-Evans," Lord Hatfield said, "I must let you try mine. Sir Richard Hilsey-Chaston gave me a set of darts which is said to be one of the best in the world."

"Is it a Winmau? That's the best I've played with."

"No, no, this was a custom board made for him by some chappie down in Suffolk. Completely hand-made, silver tipped, perfectly balanced – you won't find a better set anywhere."

"I'd be delighted, sir."

"Jolly good!" Lord Hatfield said, beaming. "Well, I must be off… I told Morely to keep the motor running, and petrol isn't as cheap as it used to be, eh what? Cheerio!"

We all waved goodbye to the old gentleman as he wrapped himself in his muffler and disappeared out the door. For a moment we all basked in the pleasant soup of happiness that Lord Hatfield had left in his wake.

"What a nice man," I remarked.

"Oh, a delight," Henry said, clapping me on the shoulder. He took a step back towards the bar and then added, "By the way, everyone – we're doing a preview performance of the show tomorrow."

There was a moment of stunned silence. Daniel interrupted with a loud whimper.

"We can't!" Nora cried.

"We just can't!" Dora echoed.

"Henry," Gladys said, approaching him with hanging lower lip, "we're not ready for this show to open!"

"Do you think I don't know that?" Henry said, his voice calm. He lifted a cigarette to his lips and let it hang there, unlit. "I've been watching this show for the past three weeks. It's an utter monstrosity."

"But what are we supposed to do?" Daniel cried. "We haven't even got all our costumes done yet!"

"We don't need them," Henry said calmly, taking the cigarette from his lips. "Look. Lord Hatfield asked very politely if we could come tomorrow night and do a quick preview performance – just a scene - for a few friends. I explained to him that we're not ready to go up yet, and he said that was quite all right. So we're going to go and do one scene, sans props and costumes, at the manor tomorrow night. That's all."

One scene. Well, perhaps that wouldn't be so bad.

"What scene are we doing?" said Gladys, ever practical.

"The one where he finds out his wife is dead."

Oh. My biggest scene – the scene with the monologue that everybody knew. Sure. It was a couple days ahead of schedule, but it would be okay. But then abruptly the room went black and I heard a loud thump.

I heard Daniel's voice say, "Is he dead?"

"Hold a mirror under his nose," Mr. Smythe's voice said.

I slowly became aware of the fact that my eyes were closed, and that the voices were coming from somewhere above me. It took me several moments to piece together the fact that the loud thump I'd heard had the floor hitting the back of my head. Did I faint? Why did I faint – oh, wait, did they say something about…A PERFORMANCE?! In front of people I didn't even know?!

Even half unconscious the thought of it made my toes curl and my stomach tangle. I think I might have groaned aloud before I opened my eyes.

When I finally did open my eyes, I found a circle of concerned faces above me.

"There he is!" Henry said delightedly. He grabbed me by the shoulder and heaved me roughly to my feet. "See! Good as new!"

"He better not do that during the show tomorrow," Mr. Smythe grumbled, looking me up and down with obvious distaste.

"Do what?" Henry cried. "That was *excitement*-fainting, wasn't it, champ?" He shook me roughly. "Look at him, he's like a prize fighter! He can't wait for the challenge!"

I felt extremely light-headed, and it must have showed.

"This is a farce," Mr. Smythe announced.

"Don't be such a bloody pessimist, Smythe," Henry said, leading me over to the nearest chair. "Jenks, get my friend here a whisky sour." He looked at his actors with irritation. "Well? What are you looking at? Go home and practice your lines!"

Slowly, uncertainly, the Oras, Daniel and Smythe went for their coats and trudged towards the door. I sat there at the table, shivering like a sick dog.

Gladys came and sat down next to me, placing her hand over mine. She smiled at me supportively.

"Gladys," I whispered, my hands shaking under hers, "I can't do this."

"You can do it," she whispered. "You're just having a touch of stage fright. Once you get out there and start saying your lines, it'll go away."

"No, no, seriously. I can't do this. I can't walk out on a stage in front of people. I'll die."

"You're not going to die, son," Henry said, appearing at my side and sliding a short whiskey sour under my nose. "Believe me – I used to feel the same way. I still get a bit goosy feeling right before I walk out on stage. Now, come on, old boy. Stiff upper and all that. Drink it down and we'll go home."

I took a tentative sip of the whiskey sour and almost gagged on it – it was all whiskey and no sour. "I think I'll pass."

"Oh? Well, I could use one myself." Henry picked up the glass and drained it in one gulp. "Put that on my tab, Jenks!"

I heard some faint cursing from Mr. Jenks's direction. Gladys put her hand over mine again and said, "Let's get you home. You can rest and regain your strength."

"Yes," Henry said, standing up and lifting me to my feet by my elbow, "let's get moving. The booze is better at my place. Goodnight, Gladys."

"Goodnight?" Gladys blinked. "Of course. At your place. It makes more sense – bed and all."

I couldn't help but notice that Gladys seemed disappointed that I was going home with Henry, but I was too sick and upset to do much about it. I managed a weak smile and murmured, "Thanks for letting me stay last night, Gladys."

"No problem," she said hastily, gathering her things and heading for the door. "See you tomorrow. Call me with the details, Henry."

"Will do, dear," Henry said lightly, throwing his cloak over my shoulders. "Let's go, dear boy. It's a good night for walking and talking."

* * *

When we reached his cottage, Henry sat me on the couch and went into the kitchen.

"You know what would be good in this weather?" Henry called. "Mulled wine."

My stomach revolted. "I couldn't touch a thing."

"Oh, nonsense. Nothing could be better for a queasy stomach than mulled wine. It'll just take me a minute…"

I heard pots banging and some sloshing. I lowered my face into my hands. Perhaps I would step out on stage, take one look at the audience, and pass out cold like I had done tonight. Of course, it could be worse -- I imagined myself up on stage in front of Lord Hatfield's fancy friends, opening up my mouth to say my lines, and vomit spraying forth like multi-colored party streamers. Or maybe… worst of all… I would step out there, open my mouth, and nothing would come out. I would struggle, and sweat, and just stand there, silently dying. There was no way out of that one. You can't improvise Shakespeare.

A warm, cinnamony smell had begun to billow out of the kitchen… It smelled like Christmas, spicy and comforting. Henry emerged happily with two steaming mugs.

"Here you are, chap," Henry said, pushing a mug into my hand and sitting down in his over-stuffed chair. "Oh, hang on a tick – let me turn on the fire and put on some music. That'll complete the picture."

He reached over and switched on his gas fireplace, which burst into false flame. Then he walked over to the ancient record player in the corner and slipped a George Harrison album onto the tray.

"There we are," Henry said, sitting down and picking up his mug. He blew at it and sipped it casually. "Feeling better?"

"Not really," I said, sipping my own. It was very strong tasting, but good. I took a deep breath and said, "Henry, I'm going to louse this thing up."

"No you're not," he said firmly. "Look at me, Matthew. Look."

I looked up at his small, square, British face. "Am I a fool?"

I hesitated. "Uh…"

"Thank you for the hesitation; that gives me a nice warm feeling. NO, Matthew, I am *not* a fool. I have been in this business for almost forty years, and when I cast a show I know what I'm doing."

"But *I* don't!" I cried.

"Oh, come now. You must have *some* theatrical experience."

"I seriously don't. I've never been on stage. Not even children's plays in school."

"Oh, come now. Everyone has a little performance experience. Think."

"Well…" I thought back. "I… I *saw* a show, once."

"Good, good."

"It was a production of *Hamlet*, actually."

"Even better!" Henry cried.

"But I didn't like it. I couldn't figure out what was going on and I fell asleep."

"Ah," Henry said, then took a long, long drink of his mulled wine. He sat back in the chair and stared at me for a moment. Then he took a deep breath and leaned over, patting me on the knee. "My lad, that just makes you unsullied and un-jaded. Believe me, you have a special... something. I noticed it right away or else I never would have cast you in the show." He got a distant look in his eyes. "You almost remind me of... me."

This distracted me completely from my anxiety. I looked up at him with wide eyes. "I *do?*"

"Quite," he said, sipping his drink again. He reached over to the coffee table for his cigarettes. "Something about you takes me back to myself at your age. Except," he added, staring distantly at his mantel, "when you were playing darts. That reminded me strongly of my father. He was a passionate darts player... Somewhere around here I've got his darts set. I'll have to try and find it."

I felt a knot form in my stomach. I was on the edge of my chair. *Could it be?* Could this be the connection I'd been looking for all along – the proof that Henry was my father? No, no, I thought, pulling back. It was not proof. It was coincidence. Lots of people enjoy darts.

Ask him. Ask him now. Ask him if he's your father. The time is right.

I opened my lips. "Henry —"

"Well, that's enough of that," Henry announced, cutting me off. He got up suddenly, turning off the fireplace and the record player. "I need to get in a quick croquet game – I'm too wound up to sleep. Care to join me?"

Cursing myself for having missed the right moment – but delighted that I was being invited to one of Henry's private backyard croquet experiences – I borrowed his cloak again and followed him out the door.

In the course of the evening we drank four bottles-worth of mulled wine and played moonlight croquet in the backyard until we were too stupid drunk to keep score. After that things get kind of hazy. I faintly remember exchanging clothes with him, laughing a lot, and throwing up behind a wheelbarrow while Henry patted my back.

I didn't become fully aware again until sometime during the night. I woke up face down on Henry's living room rug. Moving made me nauseous, so I simply opened my eyes and looked up.

Henry was sprawled across his armchair, sound asleep and snoring soundly. He was wearing my kilt and had his shirt bound up around his head like a turban. The floor around his feet was littered with empty wine bottles. There was an un-lit cigarette sticking out of his nose.

"That's my Dad," I whispered proudly into the carpet, and passed out again.

CHAPTER NINE

Cold Rain

We were to arrive a little bit before the performance to socialize with Lord Hatfield's guests. But, really, the socializing was to be kept to a minimum: we were only allowed about five minutes to mix before a butler herded us into a music conservatory to set up our scene.

In a sense, Henry's attempt to quiet my nerves the night before had worked: I was now too sick and hung-over to be worried about the show. At least, that's how it was until we walked in and set up a faux stage in the conservatory. As soon as we had arranged a stage in the corner of the room and Gladys had gone off to tell Lord Hatfield and his guests that they could watch the show, I felt a wave of lightheadedness.

Henry, who had seemed distracted, was instantly at my side.

"I can't do it, Henry," I muttered.

"Yes you can," he said. "Now break a leg."

"What does that even mean?"

He took a deep breath and then explained, rather in the manner of an adult explaining to a child that eating poison is bad, "It's considered bad luck to say 'good luck' to someone before a performance – so, instead, we say 'break a leg.'"

"Oh. So – it's kind of a code."

"In a sense. I wouldn't actually *want* you to break a leg at this point. Though a nice swift kick to the shin probably wouldn't be a problem." As if to punctuate his statement, he inexplicably kicked me in the shin with the toe of his dress shoe.

I probably would have done some colorful cursing, but Lord Hatfield chose that moment to burst in. He was followed by a crowd of his guests, who seated themselves before us in the arranged chairs.

I froze.

They stared at me.

I stared at them.

They stared at me some more.

I cleared my throat.

Daniel and Mr. Smythe looked at me expectantly. I had the first line.

For a moment I felt as if all the words I had memorized were absolutely gone from my brain. But then my leg gave a sudden throb and I remembered Henry with a burst of rage and I announced, "Hang out our banners on the outward walls; the cry is still 'They come'. Our castle's strength will laugh a siege to scorn…"

And before I knew what was happening, the entire scene had passed away, and Lord Hatfield's guests were applauding.

When I realized that it was all over, that I had successfully performed the scene, I felt an adrenaline rush like you wouldn't believe. As our small audience politely applauded and we took our bows, I found myself grinning like an idiot. I looked over at Henry, who stood in the doorway in the shadows, and gave him a "thumbs up" sign.

Perhaps, in Theatre, a "thumbs up" is the equivalent of wishing yourself good luck.

Someone shoved Henry out of the way and strode into the room. I couldn't see who it was until she reached the front where I was standing.

Sophia, dressed in a black evening gown, announced in a loud, theatrical voice, "Lord Hatfield, I *demand* that you cancel this show."

My mouth dropped open. I looked over at Daniel and Smythe, who had similar expressions of disbelief.

"My dear," Lord Hatfield said, rising up out of his chair in our improvised front row, "why would you make a request such as that? The scene we just viewed was quite good…"

"The quality has no bearing on the matter," Sophia said grandly. "I demand that you cancel this show because not only because one of the key players is a blackguard and knave who deserted a poor young woman in need… but because I have evidence that implies that the casting was based on severe nepotism. It would cast a stain on your honor to be associated with such an appalling, scandalous situation."

"What in God's name are you talking about?!" Henry cried, striding angrily up to the front of the room where we stood. He took his own spot on the stage, facing her while quarter-turned to the audience. "Lord Hatfield, I demand that you have this woman removed. She is disrupting the proceedings and upsetting my actors."

"Just a moment, old chap, just a moment." Lord Hatfield adjusted his monocle. "Let's hear what the lady has to say. Sophia dearest, what is this evidence you mentioned?"

Opening a narrow black purse, Sophia slowly drew out one of my notebooks.

I nearly wet myself.

"Lord Hatfield," Sophia said, flipping open the book to a marked page, "I am in the possession of a notebook belonging to *that young gentleman there*. In it, he states that Henry Dale Kitteridge – a man you trusted – *is his ILLEGITAMATE FATHER!!!*"

It was as if all the air was sucked out of the room.

I felt the color the drain from my face, and slowly turned towards Henry. I didn't want to look at him, but I couldn't help myself. What would I see?

His face was contorted in an expression of… confusion? Anger? His mouth was hanging open, one eyebrow raised, the other pulled tightly down. He looked from Sophia to me, then back again, before finally sputtering out, "Why, that's… that's *ridiculous!*"

"Oh?" Sophia said grandly. "Is it really?"

"Yes, it is!!"

"Oh really. Well, the facts of the matter speak otherwise. You went on a tour of America the year this young man was conceived. And this notebook states that you admit you knew this young man's mother."

"I *knew* her," Henry said, planting his hands on his hips, "but not in a *biblical* sense! She was a friend – no, not even a friend. An acquaintance."

Sophia faltered. She looked from the notebook to me, then back to Henry. "But – in his notes – this young man states that you…"

"It is impossible," Henry snapped, snatching the notebook from her hands. "Whatever this notebook says, it's wrong."

"You could be lying!"

"I'll do a lie-detector test! I'll do a *blood* test! They'll both tell you what I'm telling you right now - I am *not Matthew's father!!*"

And then he began ripping the pages out of my notebook and tearing them to shreds. He then threw the shreds on the ground and jumped on them.

This scene had obviously turned out considerably differently than Sophia hoped. Blanching, she picked up her skirts and darted from the room.

"Ladies and gentlemen!" Lord Hatfield cried in dismay to his bemused guests, "I'm terribly sorry for this… interruption. If you would follow Jennings there are desserts and drinks in the dining hall."

Seeing his guests filtering out of the room, Lord Hatfield approached Henry slowly with a distraught look.

"Henry, old boy," he said gently, "this was most embarrassing. Most."

"I must agree," Henry cried, still stomping my notebook. "I've never been so insulted in all my life!"

"But… oh dear." Lord Hatfield didn't seem to be able to finish his comment, and slowly followed his guests out of the room.

Henry tugged on his hair for a moment, then whirled around on us actors who were still standing there like dummies.

"Well?" he barked. "What are you all staring at? Show's over! Go home and run lines! Rehearsal tonight at seven!"

Smythe approached him. "Is what she said true, Kitteridge?"

"Et tu?" Henry stared him down. "No! How many times must I say it? No, no, NO!! I am not his father!"

"Well, you do kind of look alike," Dora said, thoughtfully looking from him to me. "Around the nose, I mean."

"And it was kind of funny how you promoted him to star right after he showed up," Daniel loudly remarked. "That's what I'd call *peculiar*, if you ask me."

Henry spun on us, his eyes wide with rage. "So it's come to this, then. I haven't even the trust of my own actors."

"Well…" Daniel went on, but Henry cut him off.

"That's quite enough." Mustering all the dignity that he could. "And now, if you will excuse me, I'm going to go get a drink, and see if I can salvage the remains of Lord Hatfield's respect for me."

"Henry," Gladys said meekly, trotting after him, "where are we having rehearsal tonight?"

"It's cancelled!" Henry snapped.

Slowly, the rest of the cast filtered out of the room after him, no one looking at me. Eventually, it was just me and Gladys alone in the conservatory.

She started to speak to me, but I turned and ran.

* * *

I don't think I've ever been as broken as I felt running down that road in Mosstone. The cold wind lapped at my tender vittles under the kilt as I ran, but I didn't care.

Henry was not my father.

He was disgusted – insulted – by the idea.

He didn't even really like me! All of last night – that wonderful bonding experience – had just been a sham to make me do this show! I had gone through all this stress, all this trouble and humiliation – for nothing!

I ran and ran and ran. I ran until my mouth was dry and my lungs burned like hot coals inside my chest. I ran until I found myself at the place that had started me off on this path to destruction – the church where Henry's pantomime had been performing.

By this time it was dark. The wind was beating down on me and speckles of icy cold rain were slicing across my skin. Eager for shelter, I went to the door of the church and let myself in.

An elderly couple were kneeling at the altar in the golden glow of a dozen small shining candles. Shivering in the cold that clung to me, I didn't want to disturb them. I took a seat in one of the pews in the far back of the church – then slowly sank down and lay my head on the hard wood, closing my eyes.

I couldn't think about the situation I was in. I couldn't think about Henry not being my father, or how much money I'd spent to come here – or how I had really begun to like Henry and feel glad that he was my Dad.

I felt hollowed out. My eyes stung.

After a few minutes of sitting in silence, I heard someone sit down in the pew next to my feet. A moment or two passed, and then he gently cleared his throat.

"Would you like to talk, son?"

I sat up and looked at Father Douglas's kind, white-hair-fringed face.

I tried to open my mouth, but my voice caught. I gave a long, shuddering sigh and then said, "Not really, Father. I kind of just want to be alone right now."

"I understand." He patted my shoulder, then got up and looked back at me. "I shall be in the rectory office. I have tea, coffee and cocoa, and some excellent chocolate biscuits. If you decide you would like someone to talk to – I shall be there."

He walked up the isle, genuflected before the altar, and then disappeared into the vestibule. Sitting up, I took a deep breath, inhaling the familiar smell of the church. I guess Catholic churches everywhere smell the same – a clean, musty smell of wood and incense. It made me miss home.

I became aware that someone else had sat down in the pew next to me. I turned my head, and beheld Gladys's small, earnest face staring at me.

"I thought I'd find you here," she said quietly. "I'm awfully sorry about what happened."

"It's okay," I whispered, shrugging my shoulders. "Oh well. I guess I'm going home."

She blinked at me uncomprehendingly. "What do you mean? Like, back to Henry's?"

"That's not my home," I said sharply. "My home is in Chicago. I haven't got anything here."

"But – the show…"

"Do you really think I'm going to finish the show now?" I shook my head. "Uh-uh. I'm out of here."

She looked away for a second, staring up towards the people praying at the front of the church. "So you're leaving."

I nodded firmly. "That's all that's left for me at this point."

"I see."

I didn't even see Gladys's fist until it hit me square between the eyes.

I saw a flash, and then I saw stars, then the ceiling. The next thing knew I was flat on the floor between the pews and Gladys was standing above me, shaking with rage.

"How *dare* you!" she cried.

"Crap," I said, incoherently, trying to sit up. My nose throbbed and I felt wetness dribbling down my lips. "What the hell did you do that for?"

"How dare you!" she repeated. "You liar!!"

"I didn't lie --!"

"You certainly didn't tell the truth!" Gladys cried. "You lied by not telling me *why* you wanted to be in this show. You had your own *private little plans*, and you didn't care who you upset or… or…" She struggled for words.

"Now wait just a minute!" I cried, wiping my bleeding nose on my cuff. But she went on relentlessly.

"This show depends on you – *everyone* in this show depends on you – and you're just going to pack it all in because your personal, private little project didn't work out? You're no better than Sophia! You don't even care that you'll destroy the show and destroy Henry and destroy…" She choked suddenly, tears spilling down her red little face. "I thought you were a good man. I was wrong. Go back to Chicago!   I never want to see you again!"

With that she bolted out the doors of the church.

At that moment, I had a revelation.

I scrambled to my feet and ran after her, with just a glimpse of the two very startled old people at the front of the church.

Outside, icy cold ran was pouring down from the sky. Through the driving rain, I could just see that Gladys hadn't made it very far. She was standing in the middle of the road with her head down and her eyes covered, rapidly getting drenched.

"Gladys!" I cried, running towards her.

She looked up and started to run, but I caught up with her and threw my arms around her.

"Gladys," I said, "come back inside."

"Let me GO!"

"Gladys," I cried, "I'm… I'm sorry."

When she heard that Gladys stopped struggling, and looked up at my face, which was dripping water onto hers.

"Gladys," I said, my voice lower, "you're right. You're absolutely right. I… I had no business getting involved with this production just to find out if Henry was my father. I was so focused on that I just wasn't thinking about anything else…"

"That's not an excuse!" she cried.

"It's not an excuse – just an explanation. I should have been upfront with Henry – and with you. The way I've gone about this whole thing has been downright manipulative and dishonest…"

Just like Henry, the words echoed in my head. But I didn't say that, because it no longer meant anything.

Gladys's face was growing white with the cold of the icy autumn rain that was drenching us, and her teeth chattered as she stared up at me. After a long moment of examining my face, she said, quietly, "I'm glad that you feel that way."

As I stared down at her, I realized I was feeling something else as well. Gladys was reminding me so much of Patty – of the things about Patty that had always attracted me to her. Her strength, her honesty – her ability to tell me off if I needed it. But where Patty was all prickles and sarcasm, Gladys was gentle kindness and meek honesty.

"Matthew," Gladys said suddenly, her voice childlike. "Will you stay? Please?"

I was kissing her before I knew what I was doing.

We stood there in the rain for a long time, clasped to each other, not saying a word. It wasn't until I felt her shivering against me that I realized that we were absolutely freezing. I slowly released her and took her hand.

"Father Douglas has tea and hot chocolate," I said quickly. "And I think I owe him an apology, too. Let's go inside."

Gladys hesitated at the door of the rectory, dragging me back by my hand. "Matthew?"

"Yes?"

"I love you."

I took a deep breath, knowing what I was about to say was going to really complicate matters.

"I love you too, Gladys. Now let's get inside before we die of pneumonia."

CHAPTER TEN

The Duel

I slept on Gladys's couch again that night.

Even though I spent the remainder of the night alone, it was one of the most blissful nights I have ever spent. With the now-familiar yellow blanket over me, I cuddled up against those worn cushions and smiled beatifically into them for the rest of the night.

It wasn't until I opened my eyes in the morning that some of the reality of the situation began to creep into my consciousness.

I was in love with Gladys – and Gladys was in love with me. But I was going home in a few days. I couldn't stay here. I had a job and a life back home – and I, with all my bills on auto-pay, I was doubtlessly out of money. I couldn't possibly extend my visit – nor could I take her with me.

With this dark thought, I got up and was greeted to a delicious breakfast. Now used to finding me on their couch, Mr. and Mrs. Gray greeted me kindly and asked polite questions about how the play was going.

I said it was going just fine and looked forward to seeing them at the performance.

"Oh, I do always enjoy Mr. Kitteridge's plays," the Mum said, putting a thick piece of bacon on the plate in front of me. "I laughed meself silly on that last one."

I had a moment of déjà vu. Mrs. Jenks had said something similar. I hastily remarked, "Well, I don't think this one will be quite as funny. At least, I hope not!"

Gladys had taken the day off of work. We spent the majority of the day spreading flyers, and then went home and did last-minute work on the costumes – a few buttons and frills needed to be added. When we were all done, we still had two hours before the dress rehearsal, so we had dinner and then – sleepy and full – sat on the couch whispering and holding hands like a pair of love-addled adolescents.

We were interrupted by the phone jangling loudly at my elbow. I looked up at the clock with surprise to discover that we were almost late for rehearsal.

Gladys grabbed the phone. "Yes?"

She waited a moment, listening intently to the receiver. "Yes, ma'am. I'll tell him."

"What was that all about?" I asked when she'd hung up the phone.

"That was Mrs. Jenks. She said a package had come for you and that you should come by and get it."

"A package?" I said, my eyes opening wide. "That must be a mistake. Who on earth could have sent me a package?"

"I don't know. Well, do you want to go and get it before we go to rehearsal?"

"No, we haven't got time. We're going to be late as it is."

Suddenly the phone jangled again. Gladys impatiently picked it up. "Yes?"

She listened for a moment, and the color slowly drained from her face.

"But – but – why?" She was silent for a moment, and then said, "I see."

She put down the receiver and turned her face away from me.

"What was all that about?"

"That was Henry," she said, in a small voice. "The rehearsal is cancelled."

"Cancelled?" I repeated, my mouth dropping open. "But – but this was the last rehearsal. The show is tomorrow!"

She shook her head slowly. "Lord Hatfield pulled our funding. The entire show has been cancelled."

I sat there silently for several minutes, my mind reeling. I had never wanted to do the show – but it couldn't end like this! I fingered Gladys's cold little hand in mine, and then suddenly launched myself off the couch like a missile.

"Where are you going?" Gladys asked.

"I'll be back," I shouted backwards, as I threw open the door of the house and charged into the night.

* * *

Lord Hatfield's butler did not want to let me in. I have no doubt that I looked like a freak in slept-in kilt, and he probably recognized me from the disturbance at the show the day before. Finally, I just said, "Look – tell Lord Hatfield that Matthew Evans is here and that I'd like a few words with him. If he doesn't want to see me – fine! But I want to hear it from *him!*"

With a look of distaste, Jennings shut the door on me and went to discharge this errand. It seemed like I waited hours before he finally came back and said, with a wrinkled nose, "Lord Hatfield will see you."

Jennings led me through the impressive hallway down to a small door with gilded edges. He opened it for me, and I found Lord Hatfield seated in a comfortable chair next to a fire, smoking a pipe and drinking what was probably a glass of sherry.

"Mr. Evans, sir," Jennings announced.

Lord Hatfield looked up with a smile. "Good evening, I don't believe that –" His smile suddenly faded. "Oh. I beg your pardon; I thought your name was Hatfield."

"That's my stage name," I said hastily, not wanting to waste time in explanation. I barged into the room. "Look, I understand why you cancelled the show. That display last night probably ruined your confidence in us – and in Henry. But I really think that you should give us another chance. It was a personal matter that's been settled -" (more or less true), "-- and if you'll just give us another chance, I think that tomorrow you'll be pleasantly surprised."

He took the pipe from his lips and thoughtfully tapped it into an ashtray at his elbow. He lay his pipe down and stood up.

"I'm afraid it's too late, young man. My mind is made up. As you said, that incident last night shook my confidence. I wished to sponsor this theatre company because I'm looking for a sound investment in the culture of this town. Yes, the performance you all gave in the scene from the show was sound – but afterwards, when the lady from your show came in and your... *ahem*... parentage was questioned... Well, it jolly well led me to the thought that perhaps this theatre company's parts are simply too unstable for it to succeed as a whole. To spare us all further embarrassment, I decided it would be best to simply cancel the production."

I couldn't entirely disagree with him. I lowered my eyes. "I thought you might say that."

"Well, there you have it."

"And that's why," I took a deep breath, "on your honor, I must challenge you to a duel!"

He stared at me blankly. "A... duel?"

"A *darts* duel," I said, hastily. "You said you were an excellent darts player. We'll play three sets, and we'll just say that the best two out of three wins. If I win – you let us do the show tomorrow, and decide from *that* show whether you want to become our on-going sponsor us or not. You really don't lose anything because you were going to do that anyway. And if you win – we can forget this whole thing. I'll go home with no complaint, and you can go back to your sherry with a clear conscience. Do we have a deal?"

Lord Hatfield chewed the ends of his mustache for a moment, then picked up his glass and took a delicate sip of it. "Well, as you've challenged me to a duel on my honor, I really don't see that I have a choice. I accept, and I also accept your choice of weapons. BDO rules?"

"Of course."

"Jennings, light the fire in the game room, will you?"

Lord Hatfield had a spacious game room on the north side of the manor. There was a pool table, a table-tennis table – and at the very end of the room, sequestered in a place of honor, a darts board – a wire rimmed board, the real deal.

There was a small table next to it with a flat, ebony box laying on it. Lord Hatfield opened it with a flourish and, on a pad of blood-red velvet, I beheld ten gleaming silver-tipped darts.

"Select your color, young man," he said. "You may go first."

Selecting black, I easily beat him at the first game; the silver darts, which felt perfectly balanced in my hand, thudded home into the bull with deadly accuracy. There were two that landed very slightly outside the center circle, but it didn't matter. All Lord Hatfield's shots wavered a little, and they all landed outside the center circle, one missing the board entirely. Jennings, as our referee, called the game in my favor.

"Good show, young man," Lord Hatfield said. "Jolly good show."

But I underestimated Lord Hatfield. That first game had simply

135

been a warm-up match for him: again, two of my darts were outside the center circle, but *every single one of his* thunked home into the bull. As I watched him throw, I began to sweat: this was no amateur I was dealing with. His form was perfect, his eye was perfect – and he probably had a lot more experience than I did. Not to mention that these darts had been custom made for him – probably balanced exactly to his hand.

"Game two to Lord Hatfield," Jennings said impassively.

"Good show," I said, swallowing dryly. Lord Hatfield inclined his head.

On the third and final game, a single one of his darts landed outside the center circle – millimeters outside. That meant if I played a perfect game, I would win. But I hadn't played a perfect game yet tonight. And if I played the way I had been playing, and two of my darts strayed, I would lose.

"Your move, young man," Lord Hatfield said, stepping aside gracefully. "Best two out of three, so this game will decide the winner."

I scooped up my black darts from the table and eyed the board, chewing my lip. I took my position at the white line painted on the floor, and threw my first dart.

Good. Perfect center. The second one followed suit, as did the third.

But on my fourth throw, I felt myself tense. The moment it left my fingers, I knew it wasn't flying true. The dart skewed ever so slightly, landing outside the center bull by a few millimeters.

Lord Hatfield clicked his tongue, but said nothing.

I dragged a dry tongue across dry lips, and lifted my final dart.

Everything was riding on that last dart. I may not have found my father – but I could at least save this show for Gladys, for Henry, for everyone else in it whose play experience I had loused up.

"Have mercy," I whispered, and let the dart fly.

It landed in the exact center.

I blinked rapidly for a few moments, and then both Lord Hatfield and I turned to Jennings.

"A tie," Jennings announced.

A tie?" Lord Hatfield repeated with dismay. "Dash it, that's most unsatisfactory."

A tie. A tie? What would that mean for our duel? I don't think my nerves can handle another game...

"Never mind, young man," Lord Hatfield said, sighing and clapping me on the back. "That was the most enjoyable game I've had in years. It hasn't escaped my notice that if we *had* played on points alone you would have won, so I have decided to honor our agreement accordingly. Jennings, call Mr. Kitteridge and let him know that I have decided to sponsor this performance after all."

"Yes, sir," Jennings demurred, and disappeared into the hall.

"While he's at it," Lord Hatfield said, a boyish gleam in his eye, "let's play the tie-breaker. I *must* know who would have won."

With all due modesty... I did.

* * *

With the gift of a bottle of port under my arm, I wound my way back to Gladys's house well after midnight. I glowed with satisfaction – but I couldn't suppress the gnawing sense of anxiety that grew the closer I got to her doorstep.

I was going to do a show tomorrow. And even though I had just fought so hard for the privilege of doing the show – I didn't *want* to do it. The thought of it made my stomach knot up.

And whether the show succeeded or failed tomorrow – I still had to go home to Chicago in two days. I couldn't stay here. I would have no money, and I only had a tourist visa, after all. If I stayed, in days I would be impoverished *and* illegal.

And what about Gladys? My heart felt hollow at the thought of leaving her. If I went home now… I would be going home to a bare, lonely, empty existence, devoid of color and light. I'd already passed up a wonderful woman once in my life… if I did it again, not only would I never forgive myself, I would probably never have another chance.

Her beautiful pink face beamed at me as she opened the door to my knock. "Come in, Matthew. You won't believe it! I've got the best news."

CHAPTER ELEVEN

Tomorrow and Tomorrow and Tomorrow

I allowed Gladys's excitement about the show to carry me through to the next day – and then I ignored it. Ignored the fact that I would soon be on stage (well, in a bar) performing. In front of *people*.

But there was only so much ignoring it I could do. I told Gladys I needed to clear my head and went walking out in the woods for the hour before call-time, just trying to settle my stomach. Finally, at long last, I managed to psyche myself into an emotional numbness, and headed over to the pub. They had an extra room they rented out sometimes for parties that had been borrowed for the purpose of performing the show.

I well expected to be the last person to show up. But as I was opening the door Gladys ran up behind me.

"Hey," I said, "you're late too."

"I was looking for you."

I squeezed her hand. "We'd better go in – Henry will be mad."

We waved at Mr. and Mrs. Jenks and headed into the back room. The rest of the cast was already there. I noticed that they were gathered into a small group, discussing something in low voices in a suspicious-looking manner... Oh, who cares what they could be talking about? I had better things to do than worry about their petty whatevers. I continued past to the "stage" area to make sure my handful of props were set. My stomach rumbled uncomfortably but I did my best to ignore it and just focus on the routine. Sword in place. Change of clothes in place. Fake blood in place. All good. Why weren't the others checking their props? They were going to get yelled at if they weren't ready in a few minutes...

After a few minutes Henry swept into the room, clapping his hands. "All right, people! This is it! Gather around – I'd like to have a few words with you before we go up."

He stood up on a chair and Gladys and I dutifully gathered around... but the others stayed stock still, sullenly eyeing Henry from their little group. Henry looked at them with raised eyebrow and repeated his hand-clap.

"Come come," he repeated. "There isn't any time to dally. It's almost time for the show."

It was Mr. Smythe who finally spoke.

"There isn't going to be any show."

Henry blinked at him, and then uttered a sharp bark of laughter. "Oh, really."

"We're not kidding, Kitteridge," Daniel said, presumptuously. "We're quitting the show. All of us."

The smile faded from Henry's face. His eyes slowly widened. "You *what?!*"

"You heard right," Mr. Smythe said, folding his arms. "We've discussed it. This show is a farce. It was cancelled twice. We don't have enough people to play all the characters. It's ridiculous and we refuse to be involved."

"It's twenty minutes before we open doors!" Henry cried. "You can't quit now!"

"But we can," Mr. Smythe said firmly, "and are."

Henry took a deep breath – his lower lip quivered. "*After all we've been through together...*"

"Don't give me that," Mr. Smythe snapped. "I've all seen that act before. We're through, Kitteridge – through with this farce of a performance. We're done."

The trembling stopped. Henry's eyes narrowed. "Well, then. If you're going to go, just go."

If that was reverse psychology – it backfired. They went.

Henry watched them go with a fairly astounded expression on his face. I had a feeling that this might have been one of the first times that his powers of manipulation had utterly failed.

"They can't go," I whispered, then cried out, "they can't go!"

"Well, they're gone, so I guess they can," Henry said, crisply. "I guess that's it, then."

He climbed down from the chair and with all the dignity he could muster, announced, "Well, I'm going to go get drunk – and then I'm going to jump off a cliff. Tell the advance ticket holders to see Lord Hatfield for the refunds."

He stepped towards the doors of the pub, but I snatched at his arm.

"Henry, we can't!"

He shook my hand off brusquely. "We can't what? Young man, did you not see what just happened? The CAST is GONE."

"But, but," I stammered helplessly. "But the show must go on!"

Henry sighed. "Look. Without a cast, I don't have a show. I appreciate the fact that you and Gladys didn't desert me – but it's over. I should have known that when our last full rehearsal featured potato puppets that things weren't going to pan out as I thought."

"But..." I struggled with the idea that suddenly sprang into my mind. "...But, it isn't! Gladys can run tech, I can still do the Scotsman – and you know the entire script! Can't we still..."

Henry chuckled slightly, patting me on the shoulder. "Son – and I use that term loosely – I acknowledge that I'm a great actor, but there's no such thing as a serious two-person version of the Scottish play. It would be, as Mr. Smythe so liked to put it, a farce."

"It *would*!" I cried.

He stared at me for a long moment, blinking rapidly. "You mean..."

"It would be like that day you were helping me memorize lines," I said, grabbing him by his shoulders. "We *did* a two-person version of the play that day! I did the Scotsman, you did all the other lines - but you made them funny! You had the whole cast laughing! We can do it again, just like that! I'll do the straight lines – and you can just improvise around them..."

"But," Henry struggled, "the audience is coming here to see a straight play."

"But they aren't!" I cried. "*Every single person* I've talked to in this town thinks, based on your previous work here, that it's going to be a funny show! People are coming here ready to laugh!"

Henry's mouth hung open. Suddenly his hand rose up to his chin and began to stroke it, fervently. "Well, I... a few quick changes... funny wigs... get the puppets from home..." He grabbed me by the shoulders. "Matthew – this would be rough for an established performer. You'll have to think on your feet – you'll have to guess where your lines go – you may have to improvise occasionally. Are you sure you want to do it?"

"No," I said, hoarsely. "But I will."

There was a knock at the door. Mrs. Jenks poked her red face into the room. "'Enry dear, there's folks what are showin' up already. Do we let 'em in?"

He hesitated. He looked from Gladys to me, his eyes resting on me for a long moment, as if he was judging me – trying to decide if I could do this thing or not.

Then he turned to Mrs. Jenks and said firmly, "Mrs. Jenks, allow us fifteen minutes – we left some props back at my house by mistake. When Matthew and I get back, you may start letting people in."

We ran through the streets to Henry's cottage, where he threw random things into a trunk – dresses, skirts, puppets, half a dozen painted cat statues, plants. Then, heaving it to our shoulders, we ran the heavy trunk back to the pub and stashed it in the improvised "back stage" area – part of the room that had been cordoned off with sheets.

If you think it was terrifying to get ready to do a show that is completely memorized – imagine my feelings as I waited in the wings to do a show that we were essentially making up. There was a moment, as Gladys drew the curtain aside, that I really and truly thought I was going to die.

And then I was out on stage in front of a packed house, watching Henry in a wig act out the "Bubble, bubble, toil and trouble" scene with a pair of puppets.

I simply said my lines. I played my part completely straight, abbreviating my longer speeches here and there, but playing straight. But with Henry playing every other character, embracing me as Lady Macbeth, making up lines, mugging, throwing puppets, fruits and vegetables across the stage – the audience was rolling in the aisles.

I could never do a justice to that performance in a description. It was indescribable. I don't remember a good portion of it, as I was simply trying to keep up with Henry – I knew I looked like a blundering buffoon, so guess you'd say that I worked that into my performance, shambling around like a dolt, missing my mark and having to back up, upstaging Henry so that he would have to run around me – *and the audience ate it up*. And I could feel it, the thing that Agnes had said – the "waves of energy" radiating off the audience when I did something that pleased them.

Oh, god, it was wonderful.

After the final climactic battle scene between Macbeth and Macduff – when he pulled out a starter pistol and shot me – and I collapsed dramatically to the stage, and Henry gave some kind of rough, humorous approximation of Macduff's closing speech – I looked up at him again, *and I saw him as the audience saw him – and I suddenly understood this whole acting thing.* I understood why people do it, why people watch it, and why it goes on. And, god help me, I wanted to do it again.

When we finally took our bows, the audience nearly stormed the stage. We took four bows before Henry grabbed my arm and hustled out a back door into the alley behind the pub.

"Standing ovation!" Henry cried. "Four bows! Never, never! Never in this town! Never!"

I couldn't tell if he was happy or sad – or why we were standing out in this alley. "Henry – what are we doing?"

"Oh – didn't I say? Lord Hatfield is meeting us back – oh, there you are, Lord Hatfield."

Lord Hatfield had come around the corner of the building with his butler Jennings, still chuckling and wiping a tear form his eye.

"Henry," he said, clapping him on the shoulder, "by Jove, that was the funniest show I have ever been privileged to see."

"Thank you, Lord Hatfield," Henry said, again bowing grandly.

"Of course, it wasn't at all the sort of thing that I wanted to sponsor," Lord Hatfield said, "so I won't be pursuing the project. You understand, I hope?"

My stomach lurched. I looked at Henry with wide eyes.

But to my surprise, Henry was completely unfazed.

"Of *course*, Lord Hatfield," Henry said, again bowing grandly.

"Wonderful show, old man. Just wonderful." Lord Hatfield clapped him on the shoulder and then disappeared around the corner again with silent Jennings trailing behind him.

Henry turned towards me, whistling happily. "Ah well, you can't win them all. Quick, let's get in there to the after-party."

I couldn't believe he was taking this so well. His dreams destroyed, his career ended, his last chance lost – and not a tear shed? As I followed him back into the building, I was… extremely perplexed, to say the least.

The after-party was in the main part of the pub. Our audience was there, thronging around the place, drinking, carousing. They burst into cheers and applauded when Henry and I appeared. Henry lifted his hands to quiet everyone and they fell silent.

"My friends," Henry said, in a grave voice which made me think that he was about to make an announcement about the situation with Lord Hatfield, "I have an announcement to make. Today, you witnessed something – the birth of a star. I would like to present to you our Scotsman, Matthew Evans!"

They burst into thunderous applause again. I felt my face burning hotly and wanted to leave, but I felt a small cold hand slip into mine. When I looked down and saw Gladys' little pink face gazing up at me, suddenly all was well with the world.

Henry dragged us both towards the bar where we were variously congratulated by everyone in the building. Mr. Jenks gave out a free round of drinks in our honor. Henry pushed a whiskey sour into my hand, raised his glass to mine and cried, "To you, Matthew Evans!"

I drank mine down and sat down at the bar, Gladys sitting down in my lap proudly. I squeezed her until she was short of breath, and then we sat huddled together, protecting each other from the ravages of the crowd.

Finally things began to die down, and a small, balding man in a gray suit approached us. I didn't recognize him from the town, so it somewhat surprised me when he came up and familiarly said, "Excellent performance, Matt. Excellent."

"Uh, thanks," I said, a little confused by his familiarity. He turned to Henry.

"Well, Henry," he said, shaking his hand, "it was every bit as good as you guaranteed it would be."

"Thank you. Oh, Matthew," Henry said, touching my shoulder, "I don't think you've been formally introduced. *This* is Brandon Biggs."

Then he waggled an eyebrow significantly.

I looked at him blankly.

"Call me Brandon," Brandon Biggs said, then took Henry by the arm and led him off into a corner.

"What was all that about?" Gladys whispered into my ear.

"No idea, sweets," I said, emptying my glass. "Brandon Biggs. You ever seen that guy before?"

"No." She noticed my glass was empty and took it from my hand. "Let me get you a new one of those."

I kissed her cheek fondly and she went off to find Mrs. Jenks. My attention freed, I watched Henry and Brandon Biggs conversing silently in the corner of the room. After a few minutes they seemed to settle whatever they were discussing, they shook hands, and Brandon Biggs left the pub. Henry came back over, whistling happily.

"Another round!" Henry cried. "Jenks! Jenks? Where has that man gone?"

"What was all that about?"

"It's been a busy evening – I need a drink."

"Not that. *That*," I said, pointing at the door Biggs had so recently exited through. "Who was that?"

"Brandon Biggs," Henry said, vaulting easily over the bar and pouring his own whiskey, "is a theatrical impresario. A producer. He had contacted me about a month ago about the possibility of giving me a contract – but he wanted to see something that really showed off my work before he signed me on."

"Oh. Well, that worked out conveniently for you." I looked away complacently, and then the full import of what I'd just heard flowed over me. My mouth dropped open and turned slowly back to Henry. "You – you *planned* all of this!"

"I beg your pardon?" Henry said, with mock innocence.

"I don't know how you did it. I have no *idea* – how you *planned* on your actors walking out – but you did this on purpose! You wanted to do a two-person show so that you could show off to this Brandon Biggs – but you needed somebody to sponsor it. Lord Hatfield would only sponsor a straight play with a full cast. So you launched that, and got it to fall apart, leaving us with only the funny version – the version *you* star in – to perform. And you even got *me* to suggest it, and act like you never even thought of it. This was your plan from the very beginning!"

Henry sipped his drink. "What utter nonsense."

"You don't fool me. Not *this* time. How did you do it?"

"I don't know what you're talking about," Henry said firmly, "and I shall deny it to my death."

I stared at him. How did he do it? How did he make everybody think that they were doing things on their own, when really he was framing situations so that there was no other way they could act? It was... downright *diabolical*. I leaned back against the bar and let a slow whistle through my teeth. Maybe... maybe I was wrong. It was a bit far-fetched, after all. There were too many steps. Maybe he wasn't *that* manipulative.

Or was he?

But whether it was true or not, there was still one thing bothering me.

"But how did you know I could do it?" I said at last. "I mean – really. I didn't even know I could do it. How did *you* know it?"

Henry put down his glass with a hurt expression. "Well, give an old man a little bit of credit. When I saw you playing darts over there on the night of our first rehearsal – I saw by the way you moved, by the way your timing, your balance, the confidence in your face when you threw those darts, that you could do it."

I wasn't satisfied. I looked away.

"But I didn't really know," he slowly added, "until I saw that notebook of yours one evening and realized that you had an ulterior motive for coming here. You'd been feeling me out to find out if I was your father – and I never suspected. Acting isn't some magical talent – it's like darts. You throw out lines, and if your balance and your timing are correct, they hit home and the audience believes you. *Acting is just lying well*, Matthew, and you can do it."

I thought about that for a long moment, and then said slowly, "I *guess* that's a compliment."

"Well, it's the only one you're getting from me, so you might as well enjoy it."

Gladys reappeared at my elbow. "Mrs. Jenks wants you to take this – she's worried about keeping it here any longer."

She had a yellow manila envelope in her hands, and pushed it into mine.

"Oh, I forgot about this." It was addressed to me all right, care of the pub. I lifted it to my face, trying to make out the return address. It was written in blue ballpoint pen and had smeared.

"What have you got there?" Henry asked, only half paying attention. He was looking into his drink.

"I don't know." I ripped the end of the envelope off and pulled out a sheet of white paper clipped onto an ancient, brown piece of notebook paper. Perplexed, I looked at the white letter.

> Dear Matthew, (it read)
>
> Well, idiot, I'm betting you lost your phone charger – I've been trying to call you for two weeks. I found this amongst your Mom's papers and thought it might be important to your quest. For crap's sake give me a call when you get this so that Frank and I can stop freaking out – Frank's having nightmares that your dead bloated body is floating in the English channel.
>
> Hate and punches – Pat.

I unclipped this flattering letter from the old brown notebook paper and examined it with rapidly mounting confusion. It appeared to be an old letter, written and addressed to my mother... and dated eight months before I was born.

> Dearest Ladybird,
>
> My sadness at our impending parting is as deep as the ocean that will divide us. I can only comfort myself with the thought that our parting will not be long – it should not take long to complete my affairs in Mosstone. Then I will return to you and our life together can begin. Urgently awaiting our reunion, I remain,
>
> Yours devotedly,
>
> Henry Dale Kitteridge.

I read the letter three times – four times – maybe a dozen times. When I finally looked up at Henry, sitting placidly beside me, I was white and shaking with rage.

"You bastard," I sputtered, and raggedly threw a fist at him.

Henry, even off-guard, has much better reflexes than I and easily caught my fist in his hand, looking at me with confusion.

"I *beg* your *pardon?*"

"You *bastard!*" I cried. "You lied – you lied to me!   You lied to her!"

"What are you talking about?"

"You *know* what the hell I'm talking about. God!   I can't believe that, knowing how manipulative you are, that I actually believed you! You tricked me just like you tricked her!"

"Matthew," Henry said, eyes wide, "I assure you, I have absolutely no idea what you're talking about..."

I leaned into him. My face millimeters away from his, I hissed through my teeth, "*You're my father!!*"

His mouth dropped open. "Young man, I said it before, and I'll say it again, I am *not* your father. I don't know who is, but it certainly isn't --"

I threw the letter at him. "Then perhaps you can explain *that*, Henry Dale Kitteridge of Mosstone."

Giving me a funny look, he picked up the letter, smoothed it out and held it at arm's length. His eyes sped over the words until a certain point – and then screeched to a dead stop. Abruptly, Henry Dale Kitteridge blanched. The color simply drained form his face, like whiskey from a bottle. He looked like he was going to faint. His legs seemed to go weak underneath him and he threw out his arm, support himself by snatching at the bar.

"Oh, God," he whispered. The letter drifted down from his hand to the floor and he fumbled at his shirt pocket for his cigarettes. He flew off the stool, running for the door of the pub, lighting a cigarette as he went. I stormed after him – I wasn't letting him get away that easily.

I caught up with him outside the door. Some part of me was

surprised to discover that it had snowed. My hot, moist breath billowed about me like the smoke that Henry was urgently puffing out of his lungs. I stopped in front of him and stood there, tapping a foot in the snow, arms folded. I realized suddenly that tears were just freely pouring down my cheeks. God, he looked so guilty!

"You lying…" I ran out of words bad enough to call him. "You abandoned my mother, left her frightened, pregnant and alone. You promised to come back, and you never did. You rotten, lying, two-timing son of a --"

"No," Henry said, weakly, the cigarette falling out of his mouth into the snow. "No, Matthew, no… you don't understand…"

"How can you say that?" I cried, dragging my cuff across my cheeks. "The proof is there in your hand! A letter signed *Henry Dale Kitteridge!*"

"But Matthew," Henry cried, grabbing my arm, "it's not my writing! I can prove it! I swear!"

"Oh, yeah," I said, sarcastically, shoving his hand away. "Like your word is worth anything after I've seen how you manipulate people! Yeah, it's just *some other* Henry Dale Kitteridge of Mosstone." I laughed bitterly. "How many other Henry Dale Kitteridges are there in this town?"

"There *was* another, Matthew." Henry's eyes opened wide. "My father."

I snorted – then, taken aback, I realized he wasn't bluffing. "Wait, wait just a minute…"

"My father," Henry said weakly, taking another cigarette out and trembling as he placed it to his lips, "was never a big supporter of my acting – but when I was touring America in that production of Hamlet, he got it into his head that he wanted to see his son on stage. So he flew over and spent a month over there with me in Chicago before the troupe moved on to New York. But, then, when we were getting ready to pack up for New York – he said he wanted to stay for a while longer in Chicago, by himself. While I was in New York I got a telegram from him saying something cryptic about finding what he had been looking for all his life in that town, and that he was going to go home and sell the pub and take the money and move to Chicago permanently."

Henry blinked rapidly. "But he never did, because, you see, as soon as my father got back to Mosstone, he died of a heart attack. I never did find out what it was that he'd found in Chicago that convinced him to give up his life here…" He looked slowly up at me. "I guess… I guess this *rather* solves that mystery."

My mind was reeling.

"But – but – your father must have been…"

"What, *old?*" Henry shrugged suddenly, as if he had rapidly gotten used to the idea. "Not much older than I am now. He still cut a pretty dashing figure of a man. So the old dog was going to marry Anna 'Ladybird' Johnson, eh? Come to think of it, I must have introduced them. Lucky old devil."

"But – but – but that makes me –"

The next thing I knew, I was lying in the snow, and Henry was squatting next to me, calmly smoking a new cigarette. He was quite calm by this time.

"Sorry, brother," Henry said, ashing in my hair as he ruffled it with his cigarette hand. "You went out again. You do make a habit of this, don't you?"

"What?"

"Oh, no apologies necessary," he said, sitting down in the snow beside me. "It gave me a few convenient moments to think. You know, this rather explains why you remind me of me – you *are* me. Well, half-me, anyway. Explains why you're such a mad darts player, too – must have inherited that talent from the old man." He paused for a moment. "Say, I am rather sorry about your mother, old bean. If I'd only known, I would have contacted her after Pater kicked it."

I sat up unsteadily, holding my head in my hands.

Henry nodded silently. He let out a long stream of smoke, then asked gently, "She's gone too?"

I nodded.

"I'm sorry."

"It's okay," I said, meaning it for the first time. I don't know what had changed... I mean, it still hurt... but I could deal with it now. I could talk about it – and I didn't have to ignore it or put it out of my mind to keep it from hurting.

We sat there in the snow for a long time, silently contemplating the falling flakes until Henry announced, "My lower portions are soggy and frozen, Matthew. Let's get indoors. I'll buy you a drink, and we can discuss the terms of Mr. Biggs's contract with us."

"Us?" I repeated, blankly.

"Of course," Henry said, rolling his eyes. "As brilliant as I am, I can't do our show by myself. It pains me to admit it, but I need you, Matthew. You're an *excellent* straight man."

"But – but," I stammered, my mind reeling, "I've got to go home. Tomorrow! I've got a plane ticket... My visa's up in two days...!"

"Don't worry your pretty head about it," he said, patting me condescendingly. "I had some words with Mr. Biggs about it, and he's pulling some strings to get you a work visa."

"But – but – my job! My life!"

Henry turned and looked at me like I was an idiot. Taking a deep breath, he put an arm around me and said, patiently, "Matthew, I've seen you with Gladys. Do you love that girl or not?"

I felt my Adam's apple bob in my throat. "Yes, I do."

"Do you want to stay with her? Or do you want to do what my father – what *our* father – did, and leave the best years of her life for some other man to enjoy?"

I'd already done that once, with Patty – and I did not want to do it again.

"Because if you don't marry her," he said, with a sudden, odd, gleam in his eye, "I *will*."

I lurched. "But – but you said you don't get involved with crewmembers –"

"Oh, I only told her that because I thought she was too young for me. But it turns out that's not a problem in *this* family, now, is it?"

Gladys – and *Henry?!* Oh, god. I couldn't let that happen.

"Stay here in England with her," Henry said firmly. "She's a fine, fine young woman of good, solid peasant stock. Marry her and have odd-looking children. And while you're at it, I can train you in the finer arts of our business."

"*Our* business?"

"Of course! I'll have to change the name now. Henry Dale Kitteridge Productions was fine for a single man, but now that I've got a family, I would think 'Kitteridge Brothers' or something would be more appropriate – or after Gladys joins us and the two of you pop out a couple of tots, maybe we'll just call ourselves The Kitteridge Family – although that makes us sound a bit Mafioso, or like a flying trapeze act or something. Maybe Kitteridge and Co – and then I can train the tots, too! This is shaping up to be better than having a cat! Matthew, keep up, lad."

"See here," I tried to interrupt, but Henry shushed me with a raised hand.

"Matthew," he said, sternly, "you came to England to find your family, didn't you? Well, you've found it, it's accepted you – and it's keeping you. Got that?"

Well… Henry was very manipulative and selfish, and that probably wouldn't change much. But I loved Gladys, and couldn't bear the thought of losing her. It might be an uncertain life, this acting thing, but this was a lot more interesting of a future than being an IT guy for an insurance company and living out my lonely existence having dinner with my ex-girlfriend and her husband on Sundays.

"Okay," I said, simply, and followed Henry into the building that used to be my father's pub.

-o-

Jamie Alexandre Hall

Lives in Missouri with her husband, John - and also a collie, a pug, and one stray cat. When she isn't writing comedy scripts for local television, she's generally to be found reading or avoiding house chores.

This is her debut novel with Auctoritas, also available as an ebook on Kindle at Amazon.com.

www.ingramcontent.com/pod-product-compliance
Lightning Source LLC
Chambersburg PA
CBHW051833170626
46807CB00003B/1161